THE LAST LEBANESE

Anna Simón

The last Lebanese© Anna Simón
ISBN: 9798607848828
www.annasimonescritora.com
Editorial management, graphic concept: Lorena Chávez de Gaitán
Translation: Lorena Chavez de Gaitan
Cellular phone: 503-71608764
Editing and correction: Lorena Chavez de Gaitán
Cover desing: Francisco Javier Buitrago
Editorial design: María Avilés
annasimonlibros@gmail.com

Editorial El Nahual: 503-71608764

A LITTLE OF ME...

I am Anna Simón, Salvadoran writer, graduated from the University Dr. José Matías Delgado of Bachelor of Marketing.

I currently reside in San Salvador. My passion is to write and give my readers, in addition to entertainment, a positive message through my narratives. I inspired my novels in the facts of life through my own experiences or of other people, which I end up decorating with fiction to create interesting stories.

My novels are filled with thrills, suspense and love. My published tales are: Who killed Veronika? (Spanish and English version), The House of the Cliff (Spanish and English version), The Last Lebanese (Spanish version), The Kinder–Tales of yesterday (Spanish version) and Abadón-Justice and Punishment (Spanish version).

I have participated in literary contests on Amazon, and in Bubok in Spain. I have been invited to participate in a Spanish publishing house as part of their select group of writers. I also have a very entertaining book club: "The Readers Club of Anna Simon", where we share reading and other activities related to literature. As a project I have the construction of libraries for orphans and also for the elderly.

Dedication

Like all my stories, this one is also for my family in El Salvador, as well as the one I am proud to have in Colombia.

To my husband Ricardo, which is the Last Lebanese: Your grandparents will never die, they will live forever inside the pages of this beautiful tale

This story is inspired in true events and tells much of the life of Antonio J. Abosaid and Maria Simón my husband's grandparents. To whom I keep eternal gratitude for having entrusted me with his most precious memories. Thank you love, for your trust and valuable information.

CONTENT

FIRST PART

"Not because for vanity, incapacity, or pride, but because that does not fit into your life. Close the door, change the disc, clean the house, shake the dust. Stop being who you were and transform yourself into who you are."

Paulo Coelho

In life, you have to evolve. Change the hard disk in your brain. Leave the usual environment and go out to learn something new, to also meet other people and have new experiences.

Antigua was my city, but living there, despite its immense beauty and the love of my family, it no longer made sense to me; so, I decided to leave the country and travel to Rome with no intention of returning.

But not everything you plan goes well. The dream of starting a new life in another city, it went soon. And in less than a year, I returned to Guatemala. However, fate was not so bad with me; on my return, I got a surprise, something I never expected.

On the plane to Rome, I thought about my new life, and of the love disappointment, that I went through in Guatemala, I was hoping to forget the past and buried it somewhere. Therefore, the only thing I wanted, was to be happy. I longed to be far from so many lies and deceptions.

Bad experiences sometimes chase me like ghosts, but as time goes by, they disappeared. My mother is my great friend and confidant; she does not want me to remember the past. We made the deal of not to talk any more about what happened; she was thrilled when she learned that I would go to live in another city, and told me that maybe, in the distance, I would find true love.

When I arrived in Rome, I knew I was in the perfect place. The city seemed magical to me. Then, with luggage in hand, I went for a taxi to take me to the hotel. Along the way, I felt a sense of freedom, and felt new and eager to know everything I was seeing through my path. The hotel was in the heart of Rome, just around the monumental Colosseum; and near was one of the subway stations. When the taxi pulled up, I saw a narrow four-story building, and at the main entrance, a gilded, bronze-looking door that looked ancient. In the *lobby* hanged an enormous crystal *chandelier* from the ceiling. I walked to the counter and checked myself in. After, the bellman helped me with the luggage and went to show me the room. It was small, but it had enough space for one person. There, it was a double bed and a large window, facing the main street, adorned with velvet curtains that fell long brushing the floor. The bathroom was small and in marble.

I left my luggage and went out in a hurry to walk the streets. Without difficulty, I arrived at the metro station and went to the most important tourist places.

Rome, the *Eternal City*, as they call it, welcomed me into its arms, and since the first day, I felt at home. I remembered I learned in Guatemala, about its monuments, history and gastronomy, but at this moment I would begin to enjoy this beautiful place in real life. I liked seeing the store windows, and the pedestrians who walked along those great avenues.

The day was short. My adrenaline was still running, nevertheless my body was already asking for a break; at that moment due to the time difference I began to suffer the effects of *jet lag* or *transoceanic syndrome*. I went up to my room, took a good shower, and fell asleep profoundly.

The next day the rays of the sun passed through the window and illuminated everything around me. In a semi-conscious state, it took me a little to realized that I was not in Antigua; which usually happens when one moves from a distant place and wake up in a strange bed.

Once I took a shower, got dressed and put some makeup on, I went down to have breakfast: *brioche* and *caffè macchiato.* Then I went to the counter and asked for information about the apartments for rent.

The hotel *concierge* gave me a brochure where I saw an apartment that I found convenient; it was very close to the hotel. If I wanted to start a new life, I needed a permanent place, I had come from another continent and I had no intention of returning to Antigua.

With the address in hand, I took the subway to Vía Urbana 96 and, without straying, I arrived at the place. The Italian language is very similar to Spanish and it helped a lot. The subway directions were clear, and people would answer gently when I asked them for help. As I left the station, I realized the apartment was only a few blocks away.

I could see in the distance an old building with an old, carved wooden gate. There was a bronze shaped hand attached to the large door. I took the heavy knob and hit the door with energy.

After several *toc*, the door opened as it creaked. On the threshold appeared a man who looked at me with curious eyes, I then asked him, with a shy voice and with my incipient Italian, if they rented an apartment there. He looked at me from head to toe and told me, I had reached to the right place.

The mysterious man introduced himself as Vincenzo Andreotti, and with a subtle smile, I told him my name was Vera and that I was interested in renting the apartment advertised in the brochure that I carried in my hand.

He was a tall and handsome man; with brown eyes, black hair, bushy eyebrows, aquiline nose, sensual mouth, and a muscular body. His voice had a marked Roman accent, the one that drags the words when speaking. Without taking my eyes off me, he invited me kindly to enter, while he was attending a telephone call. I waited without moving from there, following his instructions consciously. The apartment he showed me was on the first floor, at the end of the hall. When we were in front of the entrance, he began to ask me things that were not related to the rent, but I thought he was trying to be friendly and chatty.

He commented me he was the owner, and somewhat annoyed, said to me it was a coincidence that he was there at that moment since the manager was getting married and he had not left a replacement to help him in the building with the needs of the tenants.

Upon entering the apartment, I could see a long narrow lobby. There, was an ancient golden mirror hanged on one of the walls, and two waiting chairs rested on a red oriental rug. A few steps away, on the left side, I entered in a room where there was a sofa and two armchairs that seemed recently upholstered; there was a wooden table in the middle, and in the background, in a narrow space a fully equipped kitchen. When leaving the room, on the right side, I found two bedrooms with their bathrooms. Which, curiously, were larger than the dormitories. The apartment was simple, but it had everything I needed; so, I didn't hesitate one second to rent it and to move right away.

The day after I moved, Vincenzo visited me with the excuse of knowing if I needed something else, so I invited the *padrone di casa*, as the owner of the property in Rome is called, to sit down without having more than a glass of water to offer him.

The conversation started all over, he was flattering and expressed all kinds of compliments. I thought I didn't make a mistake in choosing Italy to change my environment. I was sure, I would always feel beautiful in Rome.

Without any prologue or shyness, he invited me to lunch and after, he will show me the city. It seemed a good idea to accept a native tour guide.

After an hour, Vincenzo knew my whole life; he had insistently inquired me about it. Talking with him was like being with a priest in a confessionary. After some time, he left somewhat in a hurry, but he said he would call me the next day.

When I woke up, I opened the window and right in front of the room, there was a beautiful and colorful orange tree, the light filtered through its branches and attenuated the sun's rays. I stretched my arms as if wanting to touch the sky; and I said out loud: *Buongiorno Roma*. I was happy. I felt safe and full of peace. I had nothing to fear. The people did not know me. The anonymity I was in gave me a sense of freedom. Then, I waited for my new friend to go to lunch.

Upon my return to the apartment, when I finished organizing everything, I was overwhelmed with fatigue and fell asleep. After sometime, I took a shower, and I got dressed, I was eager to walk the city. Already, this new-comer girl went out to roam the streets of Rome as if she were the Queen of the world. It seemed that the city was kneeling at my feet. ––I thought.

I went to visit the Roman Colosseum; I couldn't believe I saw one of the Seven Wonders of the world. The amphitheater was of the epoch of the Roman Empire, in the year I d. *C.* and in its sands had run the blood of brave gladiators and innocent Christians who had been slaughtered without mercy for believing in their God. That made me realized about how unfair life was, but that belonged to a very distant past.

Upon arriving at the building where I was living, Vincenzo came into my mind for a brief moment. I liked his figure; also, his face, and the gentle way of speaking to me with kindness. There was no doubt that he had caught my attention. He was a very sexy Roman.

As soon as I entered, the phone rang and, coincidentally, it was him. Maybe I had called him with my thoughts. After greeting me, he asked me about my day and he wanted to know if everything was fine with the apartment. He invited me to lunch again, and to visit some interesting places. It's was a good idea. We agreed to meet at noon in a small *cafe* next to the building.

When I arrived at the coffee shop, the bar counter was full. It appeared that nobody worked in that city. I thought it was great to see so many people chatting as if they were on a feast. Five minutes have passed, when I saw him enter. He was wearing a blue shirt, black pants, and around his neck, a white silk scarf. He walked to where I was and greeted me effusively with the usual two kisses, one on each cheek. He observed me closely, from head to toe, and told me I looked pretty. Everything was perfect. It was a lovely day, and the weather wasn't cold. Vincenzo's company encouraged me a lot; I had a handsome man by my side in a charming city; I couldn't ask for more.

After two *expressos*, we left the cafe and I followed him like if I were his pet. I waited to see a car parked, but instead, there was a Vespa motorcycle. Once seated, I approached his body and grabbed his waist tightly, my skin bristled. My legs brushed his, and it caused me a certain excitement. At that moment, I remembered that famous and classic Italian film, *An Adventure in Rome,* in which a girl travels on a Vespa throughout Rome accompanied by her great love; If I remember correctly, the main actor was the handsome Troy Donahue. Everything was so unexpected and unreal.

The city blended with a past full of ancient art and modernity of the present. The squares were of unparalleled beauty. When we arrived at *Piazza Navona,* I couldn't hide my astonishment at that elegant place; It had three magnificent fountains with amazing sculptures. We walked through the square until we arrived to a pizzeria that, according to Vincenzo, was the best in Rome.

––*Ciao Vincenzo!* –The owner of the place greeted him–, how is it possible that you do not introduce me to your friend? *Lei é molto bella,* ––he said mischievously.

After the compliments, we sat at a table, and there we joined a couple of charming Dutch people. When leaving the *pizzería,* Vincenzo told me there was still a lot to see, and winking, he added:

––¨Rome was not built in a day¨.

We arrived a little later than seven at night, and I invited him to come inside to have a glass of wine. When

I entered, I felt the place already had life itself and a lot of my personality. The scent of the orange tree flooded all over the space. We talked about everything, except about my past, even though some memories came to my mind without me wanting.

I told him that the most important thing was to learn the language, since I felt lost, if I couldn't speak well. He then gave me the phone number of a friend who taught Italian to foreigners. During the conversation, we talked about my journalism studies and of my passion to write stories. I also told him with enthusiasm that I loved traveling. Vincenzo told me:

––Vera, I love your simple personality, your exotic face, your brown skin, and your beautiful figure. I cannot believe that I knew you thanks to the irresponsibility of my employee. Maybe, I'll send him a beautiful wedding present, ––he said jokingly. And continued:

––Vera, I intend to help you. I don't want you to start this adventure by yourself. I will protect you so nothing happens to you.

I was a bit surprised at that fatherly attitude. However, I thanked the universe for having such a special friend by my side. I had started on the right foot. ––I thought to myself.

*****

The next day, I got up feeling confident, I went to the bathroom; and when I saw myself in the mirror my face looked tired, but inside of me there was a heart full of hope.

Around eight o'clock at night, Vincenzo Andreotti arrived and took me to a restaurant near the *Piazza de Espagna,* where there was a fashion show. Seeing something like that was a novelty to me. They were presenting the new spring collection, and the most famous Italian designers strolled proudly among of the crowd.

Once it finished, we went for a walk along the *Via dei Condotti*, and while we watched the windows of the shops, Vincenzo insisted on buying me a dress, I didn't know if I should accept it, I barely knew him and did not want to feel compromised. He insisted so much that I ended taking his offer. We entered into a Versace store; and after a while, I left the famous place with a silken garment of bright colors that adhered to my body like a second skin.

The chatter of the people was heard everywhere. On the streets, tourists came and went carrying shopping bags. Some couples walked with their babies in strollers. The children were running all over, trying to escape their parents' control. Lovers were not missing. It was a cheerful and vibrant environment.

The night became magical when we entered the restaurant and I caught the attention of everyone there. Vincenzo, noticing they were not taking my eyes off me, became uncomfortable. Embracing me as we walked, he sent a clear message that he was my owner.

The place was a typical Italian restaurant with tablecloths of the Italian flag's colors. It was full of tourists and locals.

The days went by and I felt better every time. My friend was intense, he called every morning, and every night. There was nothing yet between us, but soon the inevitable would happen. Deep down, I wanted it, but when I remembered my love nightmare in Guatemala, I would panic. I still needed more time to heal my wounds.

One morning I called the Italian teacher that Vincenzo had recommended to me. Carmen was a Spanish girl who had been residing in Rome for some time. She arrived punctual, and after the first hour of class, we had coffee and chatted as if we were old friends. She told me that as soon as she arrived in Rome, she met a boy from Ostia, and after six months of courtship, they got married; but, her marriage failed, when she knew he had lied to her. The man had a family, who he was hiding. I felt sorry for my teacher; she was an excellent instructor and a friend.

I told her that I was dating Vincenzo to what she advised me to be careful not to ended heart brokenly.

––They say they love you and want to share a life with you, but many are unfaithful, and also liars ––she warned me.

I did not want to be influenced by her comment, so I went ahead with my plans. At the end of the intensive course, we agreed to see each other again. Sometime later I called her, but my friend told me she was busy preparing her trip back to Spain.

*****

I liked Vincenzo, but I did not want to get involved with anyone, I wanted to have a bit of freedom, and my inner self was refusing to accept a commitment; however, I did not want to close the doors to love so I decided to follow his game.

Time passed quickly, and I had to look for a job. The money I have was not going to last forever. Although, I did not speak Italian well, there were always positions where there was no need to talk too much. I could work as a waitress, or in a grocery store in the cash register, where I would only need to count the money and say: *Grazie* and ciao.

Every day I checked the job offers in the local newspapers; of *Il Mattino* and *La Repubblica*, but I couldn't find nothing; so, I decided to go to an agency and handed my *curriculum vitae* to the person in charge. The girl called several places to make appointments for me, I took a seat and waited for her news. Shortly after, she gave me the details and addresses of the stores in which the interviews would take place; some of them were of prestigious designers. After a few days, my phone rang, the call was from D'Angelo, an exclusive shoe store in *Via dei Condotti*. I was so happy, with a big smile I took my bag and left. When I got to the store, a woman interviewed me briefly, and after a few minutes she asked me to come to work the next day.

Excited, I called Vincenzo to tell him the good news. He congratulated me, and immediately said to me he would have to go to inspect the place to make sure everything was fine. I felt a bit intimidated, but I decided not to take it badly; thinking that he just wanted to help me.

During my first day of work I felt nervous; however, as time went by the fear disappeared. The only thing it gave me some anxiety was an overly protective attitude of Vincenzo. He was always calling me to the store and my boss did not like it. I was nervous about losing my job.

When I returned home, at night, I felt desolated and sad; I considered my relationship with Vincenzo was going to be a problem.

Lying on the sofa, I began to meditate on his attitude,

when suddenly the doorbell rang. It was him, with a giant rose bouquet. He about to cry. He offered me an apology and swore he will not bother me anymore with his frequent calls. Seeing him so sorry, I forgave him. He pounced on me, and began to kiss me passionately, love and desire sprang up. Vincenzo stroked my whole body, and between gasps of excitement, made me some promises of love. When I less thought, was already in bed with him; the inevitable would happen. I did not regret it for a second. He was a fiery lover, full of passion.

The next day he approached me and filled me with kisses. After, he went to the kitchen to prepare breakfast, which took me to bed. I felt like a queen. With words of love and a thousand caresses, he asked me to take a shower with him. I have no way to describe everything he made me feel. The water was falling all over his chest; spreading the drops on his sex and his well-formed thighs. I assaulted by the desire to taste every inch of his body without leaving a single free space. His agitated breathing was mixed with mine, and when he kissed me again, I wanted to have him inside of me to make him explode like a volcano.

The only thing that worried me was he was so intense and somewhat obsessive with everything he did. As for love, it seemed nothing was enough for him, but I deduced it was the typical attitude of a man in love.

*****

The next day, as soon as I saw the clock, I jumped out of bed; I ran to get dressed so I would not be late for work. My overprotective lover said he would accompany me to work and would continue to do so every morning. It was a bit suffocating. But I was sure his love was heartfelt and with time it would appease. I thought I was a little ungrateful with everything he was doing for me, so I tried not to give it any importance.

Everything was going very well in our relationship; nevertheless, Vincenzo seemed not to trust me. He was always asking me questions that showed jealousy and suspicion, but for the sake of love, I tried to play along.

*****

Rome was captivating. Each day it passed; I fell more in love with that city. At work, I belonged to a lovely group of friends; in which there was a girl from Honduras, named María Elena. We both had the same culture, which made it easier for us to understand each other, and for our friendship to flourished and blended. Sometimes, after work, we would go together to have a coffee, and we talked until our tongues got numbed and there weren't any more topics to discuss. It comforted me to know I had a good friend.

María Elena had been living in Rome for a long time. She had come to Naples for a vacation to the home of a relative, and when she got acquainted with the city, she loved it so much that she ended up working there. As for her love life, she had also been deceived and did not want to know anything about it. We amalgamated a lot because of our work, she was single and disappointed in love, so my company helped her to shovel her loneliness and give her encouragement.

One afternoon, while at the bar, Vincenzo came out of nowhere, he looked angry, and yelled at me:

––Vera, how is it possible that I ignore what you are going to do after work?! You know I exist! I could've thought you had an accident or something terrible had happened. You have no consideration! --He said within a strange look.

Maria Elena, with a stern expression on her face, was stunned.

--I did not tell you, where I was-- I answered, --because we only came for a cup of coffee. What's wrong with that?

When he heard me, and noticed I was upset, he tried hard to change the tone of his voice and to control his nervousness.

--Come on. Sit down and have a coffee with us, --Maria Elena said.

He immediately sat down like an obedient child, and his rigid expression became sweet. I saw him a little embarrassed, and he explained to me he could not spend time with us because he had to go to buy a spare part for the Vespa motorcycle and feared to find the store closed. He looked stressed.

Maria Elena had more experience, than I did, with Italian men, thanks to the fact that she had been living in Rome for years, for that she warned me they were too jealous and possessive. She insisted I should be cautious to not let things pass one more step.

--What do you mean? --I asked.

--I mean that, maybe next time, he will not let you leave your house. Then, the worst will come: he can hit you and who knows what else.

Maria Elena in a worried state, said goodbye to me. I appreciated her support, and above all, to tell me with sincerity what my eyes couldn't see at that moment. It's why they said that love was blind.

I looked for an excuse to justify Vincenzo's behavior; I told myself that love was not perfect and relationships had to mature. I hoped with over time, that episode would not happen evermore. When he arrived at the apartment, he offered an apology, and I accepted it. Then we made love like never before and feeling so satisfied; my doubts disappeared as if they had never been in my mind.

*****

The day promised a radiant sun, and we decided to go to the beach, we would take with us a good *Chianti* wine and some *paninis*. Seated on the beach he again apologized for behaving like a jealous teenager. I smiled at him with a bit of bitterness and forgave him all over again.

We laid on the sand. We kiss with passion; I was exploding with desire. We try to calm our lust and craving to love by eating our *panini* accompanied by the excellent wine. Suddenly, that man, for no reason, became an angry person, out of control, I couldn't recognize him, irascibly shouting at me, asked:

––Tell me the truth! The other day that you went out, did you see someone? I know it was just an excuse to getaway. Where the hell did you go?!

After that annoying accusation, I was perplexed; I did not know if he was talking seriously or not. I tried to calm myself and answered:

––What are you talking about? Who would I see?

Later, I became stressed and heartbroken. I explained to Vincenzo, without having to do it, that I remembered keeping the receipt of the place where I went.

Nervous, I opened my bag and took it out to show it to him. Vincenzo snatched it from my hands with rudeness; when he scrutinized it, he realized I was telling the truth, then he offered me an apology, once more. In a rage, I grabbed the receipt from his hands and busted in tears.

Vincenzo changed his mood unexpectedly, which reminded me of the famous novel, *The strange case of* Dr. Jekyll and Mr. Hyde. I asked God not to be my case. It was difficult to be with him, but he was all I had at that moment. My life was going through a radical change, and I did not know if I could manage it alone. I still felt insecure and vulnerable. I did not want to experience the horrible feeling of abandonment and loneliness.

When we returned to the apartment, he prepared an exquisite dinner that took to my bed on a tray, everything adorned with sweet words and a flower he picked from out of the window. I immediately put aside the problem. I went to kissed Vincenzo, and I assured him nobody else existed but him. In the middle of the tortuous situation, we ended up making love, putting out the fire- we had started on that Mediterranean beach.

After love, the doubts visited my mind. I knew it was not normal behavior, but love was making me blind. The heat of his body, his touch, and the endless nights of passion had me tied up to him, I desired to be with him all the time. His generosity was immense; whatever I wanted, he put at my feet in a second. Being with him was like touching the sky to fall down to hell afterward. I was in a trap that I could not escape, and I did not want to. Our love had bright and dark days. Although it was a complicated relationship, I was sure he loved me. I would fight for that love until the day my nerves and my patience succumbed.

We were in the bedroom chatting about what was happening in the city when all of a sudden, he started shouting at me:

--You're a whore!

It was the first time his mouth said that horrible word and insulted me in that way. Not being enough, he continued:

--I know everything! Do not deny it! You're sneaking out with one of those guys who work in your store. You are behaving like a bitch!

When he finished, I burst into tears; I could not bear to have him distrust me again, and also insulted.

--I will not take this from you, anymore! --I shouted at him. I won't allow you to continue to disrespect me! You've already gone too far! Get out of here immediately; I do not want to see you again! --I yelled at him furiously. I was out of control.

Vincenzo, seeing me like that, became worried, and as always, he went from anger to crying and asked for forgiveness, he excused himself of his behavior for having suffered during his life. He promised me he would visit a psychiatrist to solve that problem.

After a while, I saw him calm, quiet and thoughtful. I got into my bed, I turned my back on him, and unable to sleep, I pretended to do so.

When I woke up, my face looked tired, and my hands were shaking. I looked like a drugged addict. There was the man I adored, waking up with a big smile, a very different one from the previous night. I said, good morning coldly. I got ready to go to work, and as always, he accompanied me.

On the way to the store, there was no conversation, only a spectral silence; I had no desire to speak to him, I felt so much contempt for him, that I was scared.

That night he invited me to dinner at my favorite restaurant. He wanted me to forgive him, according to him, it was a way to offer apologies. Once we would finish dinner and were about to retire, I was going to ask him to leave; I did not want to be with him anymore. I could not live like that. I felt harassed all the time and mistreated. He always doubted about my fidelity, insulted me, and then asked me for forgiveness.

The waiter arrived with the menu, and when he left, I said:

––Vincenzo, I ... I love you, but we cannot continue together. It is a decision that I have been thinking about for some time. I cannot be with a man who doubts so much about me, insults me and denigrates me in that way. Do you understand?

––What...? Have you gone crazy, Vera? ––He said, with tears in his eyes.

––I adore you; I couldn't live without you! I know I made many mistakes, but everything has been because of love. I'm crazy about you. Can you understand? I promise you; I swear to you on my mother's grave, may she rest in peace, that I will change. I swear! Give me another chance, Vera, I beg you!

When he finished speaking, I noticed he was containing his crying. I felt pity for him, and I thought that I did not understand him, maybe it was me who had to change. I could not think clearly. When I saw him so repented, I forgave him, as I had done it many times. We went out of the restaurant embracing each other, and with the desire to be together. In front of the door of the building, he held me tightly to his body and began to kiss me with despair. We entered. He did not wait to arrive to the room to undress me; at the instance, he assured me that he did not want to lose me. With those arguments, he convinced me, and we made love in the narrow space of the vestibule. The night became endless and intense; after so much sex, my body could not take it anymore.

Upon arriving at the store, Maria Elena saw me so happy that she asked me if he had asked me to marry him; I joked at her that she would be my maid of honor. The day continued without incident. My heart was filled with faith, without suspecting what awaited me.

*****

The Italian celebrated the *Festa Della Repubblica.* On that day we went out with some friends to commemorate the event. The restaurant was full, in the midst of eating, and with a silly excuse asked me to go out with him for a moment. We left the group and apologized to them. Being outside of the place, he grabbed my forearm in a roughly way, squeezed it, and cornered me in the passageway adjacent to the restaurant; the people who passed by could not see us. I was alone with him in that narrow, dark place, and in fear, so I asked Vincenzo angrily, why is that we had left our friends and what what's going on. Without answering and ruled by hatred, slapped at my face. I put my hand on my battered cheek, and I wanted to cry, however I tried to contain the crying. He looked furious and scared at the same time. I begged him to let go of my arm, and immediately I returned to the table as if nothing had happened.

No one suspected, except Maria Elena, who, noticed my red cheek. After, she asked me to accompanied her to the bathroom. There she interrogated me as if she were the police. As I told her what happened, she became pale. She, enraged told me that I had to get him out of my apartment. She wanted to know why he had slapped me, but not even me knew the reason. I I told her we would discuss the matter, the next day. Maria Elena, indignant, pointed out to me:

––Next time he will kill you, Vera! You must stop this abuse immediately!

I perceived she felt sorry for me; caressed my face to comfort me, and disgusted returned to the table. When he saw Vincenzo, he gave her a menacing look; to make him understand her friend was not alone.

We left the place without saying a word; without embracing as we walked, I refused to come near him. When we arrived at the apartment, I busted into tears, and he did the same. Seeing me out of control, he explained to me he had had a jealous outbreak. I yelled at him to leave me alone. His face went pale, and without saying anything, he grabbed his suitcase and started packing to leave my apartment. I was sad I thought it would have been better to accept for him to go to a psychiatrist, but it was too late. I did not know if he would return.

When I woke up, my face and my eyes were red by crying; the fight had been tough. I felt abandoned to my fate. In the store, I was still thinking about him. The idea of returning to my apartment and knowing I would not find him drove me crazy. Maybe it would be better if I visit the psychiatrist myself, maybe I wasn't as sane as I thought.

However, my primary doctor became my friend María Elena, who helped me to deal with the pain, the depression and to make my days of solitude less painful. She always would be with me after work and listened to my complaints without getting tired. She underwent my crying as an abandoned child and consoled me. At one point, I thought it would be best to go back to Guatemala.

*****

After a month, Vincenzo, called again. As soon as I heard him, I wanted to hang up, but he begged me not to so. With an upset voice he told me he was very depressed and his life without me made no sense.

—Vincenzo, our relationship became stormy and can no longer be. Now I want to be alone, —I said, trying to convince him.

—Why do you insist on destroying my life? —I claimed him sobbed. I ask you not to call me again, please, —and without waiting for his answer, I hung up.

After that brief conversation, I tried to control myself. I had to be strong and not give in; I was too susceptible to the pain of others.

Vincenzo did not communicate with me again. The few calls came from Maria Elena, who was still caring for me. Now we both were single and accompanied each other. I was no longer afraid to greet someone on the street, or if a young man would come over to invite me for a drink. I didn't have to hide from anyone; I was free like the wind. At least it was what I thought, but then I recognized that the memory of Vincenzo still remained engraved in my heart.

It hurt me to think that we had a lot in common and that we could have been happy, if it wouldn't be for his sickly jealousy. I entered the building and went up to my room. I saw a letter on the floor. I opened it with anxiety, it was from Vincenzo:

"Vera, I know you do not want to know anything about me, and I do not blame you. I do not want to be in this world if I'm not part of your life. I'm living in hell without you. I do

not think it's worth continuing like this. If I cannot see you anymore, I'd rather die. I only ask you to understand me and forgive me. I never wanted to hurt you, I fell in love with you, and I was afraid of losing you. Don't you understand its all about love? Only love! I'm living in the same place, and you have my number. Please call me; I want to hear your voice one last time. I beg you! I ask you to have mercy on me!"

Vincenzo

I was petrified. I couldn't even open the bag to get out the key; when I finally did, it was hard for me to open the door, because my hands were trembling. As I entered my house, I went straight to the kitchen and drank some water to pass the saliva that was stuck in my throat. I was extremely worried. I could not understand it. Would he be able to kill himself? I didn't know how to disperse that doubt; but if that happened, I didn't want to carry his death in my consciousness. I had to stop it, to do something, immediately. I called him without going over the matter. He answered me soon.

––I'm Vera, ––I said, trying to hide my anxiety.

––Vera, I was waiting for your call. I knew you wouldn't abandon me. I feel very depressed. Sorry if I don't greet you in a more effusive way.

––I received your message and I worried about you. Listen, Vincenzo: don't commit a madness! I beg you.

––Vera, I'm determined, ––he said in a barely audible voice.

––Do not do anything. Wait for me to come. Don't move from there!

––Vera, it's useless. Forgive me!

––I'm going to hang up, Vincenzo. I will ask for a taxi

and be there as soon as possible.

I left my house and hurried to go to his apartment. I rang the bell, in despair. I didn't take my finger off the button. No one opened. I panicked thinking I had arrived late. I bended down almost lying on the floor, to see through the crack of the door, but it was not possible to observe anything, only the natural light that came through it.

I was about to call the police when I heard some approaching steps and, after a few seconds, Vincenzo opened the door. He looked emaciated and dirty. I hurried to get in, pushing him. I told Vincenzo in an anguished voice that I would not allow him to commit such a madness. He did not answer anything. His face portraited the tension he was going through. Everything in his apartment was out of place. There were dirty dishes and unwashed pots in the kitchen. He had not done any cleaning; It looked like the home of a vagabond.

—Please, let me help you, I beg you. Tell me, how?!

—I don't know, — he replied.

After a brief silence he could no longer contain himself and exploded in tears.

—Don't worry, —I said, — we're going to search for help, we're still on time to solve this problem, you'll see that everything will be all right.

I went to the kitchen to make him a cup of coffee. He drank it with docility. I told him to go to take a shower; he smelled really bad. At that moment I called my work that day, I wasn't going to attend the store. Giving them the excuse that I was sick; after all, it was true, as I was beginning to feel nauseous. I spoke with María Elena to ask her the favor to cover me in the job, I could notice she was surprised and, in her voice, there was some fear.

––Where the hell are you, Vera?

––I am in Vincenzo's apartment.

––What are saying?! Are you crazy?!

––No, I was just saving his life. He wants to commit suicide.

––Do you believe him?! She said angrily.

––If you would see him, you would believe him. Trust me ––I added.

––Vera, I know you're not stupid, I to trust you, but be very careful with what you do. For now, take care, my friend!

––Okay, I promised. ––Then I hung up.

Vincenzo came out of the shower, shaved and clean. At least he already had another appearance. I asked him to go to a psychiatrist, as he had told me once, however, he watched me and remained silent. After a few seconds he said he had a friend who was a doctor and he would soon make an appointment; he begged me to accompany him. I agreed. A feeling of guilt invaded me at that moment for having allowed that night to leave my apartment; Fortunately, I had arrived just on time to save him. He went to his bedroom. He asked me not to leave him alone. Then he closed the door. I lay on the couch, exhausted and nervous.

The next day I saw him the same. The scene had not changed; that I was there, did not solve the problem, so I returned home feeling worried and responsible for his life. I called Maria Elena to calm down.

I arrived at the store early. I had huge dark circles under my eyes. My boss, with a pitiful expression, advised me to take another day off. I assumed she saw me with a sick expression.

*****

The time had come to go to the psychiatrist. I went for Vincenzo's to his apartment and felt a great relief when the door opened at the first *ring*. He looked clean and lively. His voice was different and he even smiled at me.

––Ready? ––I asked.

––Yes, Vera, I am.

––Who is the doctor? ––I questioned him.

––He's an old friend, his name is Fabrizio Gallo."

––Very well! Where is the office? ––I said.

––It's very close to here, we can walk.

I saw him so happy. I could not believe that one day before he had attempted suicide. He told me his friend was one of the best psychiatrists in Rome, and that eased my despair.

––I've known him for a long time since we were children.

Although I believed him, it seemed strange to me that if they were close friends, he would not have introduced him to me before. But that wasn't important at that moment, so after a couple of blocks we arrive at a decolored building.

The apartment was number 32. A man a little younger than Vincenzo opened the door for us and introduced himself as Dr. Fabrizio Gallo. When they both saw each other, they greet with a tight strong and prolonged hug, then the doctor asked me if I was Vera, his girlfriend. I remained silent and only shook his hand, without giving him any explanation. The office only had two rooms; there was also a small kitchen in the background. We entered directly into Dr. Gallo's office; there was only one table with two armchairs. I did not understand why the office lacked waiting chairs and a secretary. Doctors always had them.

Fabrizio was friendly and a gentleman. He informed us that he was moving out of the building and because of that he did not have much furniture in his office. He, then, apologized for the fact. I felt more relaxed, since his explanation made sense and cleared my doubts. Then he addressed at me saying:

––I have to tell you, Vera, that this man you see here, is one of my best friends and I want to see him healthy. You are the most suitable person for him to get ahead with his problem. You, Vera, are his best medicine for him ––he said with a serious expression.

After what I heard, I felt I was going to carry the world on my back, but I had promised to take care of him before God, and also in front of them.

––It will be better, ––Vincenzo said–– If I move into your apartment. You'll be more comfortable and I will feel better.

I stayed silent at such a proposition and my eyes widened open; if at that moment I had looked myself in a mirror, I might have seen a very scared woman. However, my love won the battle against my judgment and I accepted without objection.

A minute later, we said goodbye to the doctor to whom I asked for a card, he told me that he could not give it to me because he had them in the other building. After leaving Dr. Gallo, we headed to Vincenzo's apartment to collect his things. On the way I asked him why he had lied about our relationship. He apologized with the excuse that it made him feel safer.

In front of the building's gate, he thanked me so many times it bored me. Vincenzo entered my house with a happy face and his depression vanished like smoke. His metamorphosis was miraculous.

I was very clear when I told him he had to sleep in the other bedroom. I didn't feel ready to have him so close.

A couple of days passed without news, and I continued with my routine. María Elena was upset, because of my decision; she told me, insistently, that I would regret it.

Being in the apartment I had never seen where Vincenzo kept his medicines, moreover, I had never noticed he took them. Since I wanted to respect their privacy, I did not insist on knowing where he put them. Besides, I assumed he was taking them, because his mood had improved. I was calmer and did not question myself as before. Again, my heart was filled with hope.

After a week, while walking toward my house, I passed the building where Fabrizio's clinic was located, I assumed it was a good idea to go up to greet him. I went up to the third floor and rang. No one opened me. I kept insisting. I was about to retire, when I saw a woman coming out of the adjoining apartment and asked her:

—Excuse me, has Dr. Gallo moved already?"

—Who ... is Dr. Gallo? —She asked with an expression of surprise.

—The psychiatrist who has his office here, — I replied.

–You've must have the wrong building, not a single doctor lives here, that apartment belongs to Mr. Vincenzo Andreotti, and it's been empty for some years; I know it because I am his tenant too. Are you interested in renting it?

—But it cannot be. I met Dr. Gallo here last week.

—*Madam*, don't insist. I am telling you there is no

Doctor Gallo in the building.

Vincenzo had lied to me and set me a trap. It seemed that Dr. Gallo did not exist. Surely, he had mounted that charade to manipulate my feelings.

How could he have lied that way? Would he have used his friend to play the role of a doctor? Now I understood why there wasn't a waiting room or a secretary. Everything was as clear as water. There was no doubt, Vincenzo was a scam artist.

When I left the building, I went to a bar to have a *whiskey;* I needed something strong to calm down. I drank it in one gulp. I asked for another before I left. Liquor made me the desired effect. Already more sedated, I decided to face the impostor who was ruining my life.

Upon arrival, I sat in the living room. Anger had taken hold of me. Now more than scared, I was furious. As soon as he entered, I pounced on him and began to punch his chest with my fists. I was out of control.

––You're a damn liar! ––I yelled.

––What's the matter, Vera? ––He asked with an innocent expression.

––I demand an explanation, immediately! ––I shouted.

I could see his face became livid and his eyes got watery. He collapsed on the couch without being able to articulate a word.

––Tell me, who the hell is Dr. Gallo? I found out the guy doesn't exist! You have played with my feelings and my pain. You are a scoundrel!

––Just let me explain, ––he pleaded.

––You don't need to. The woman who lives next to your apartment or the supposed office of that man, has told me everything.

--Who are you trying to fool, Vincenzo? Do you think I'm stupid?

--Forgive me, Vera!

--Again?! I shouted.

With a broken voice, he told me that he was desperate and he did not know what to do to call my attention. He also assured me that he didn't want to hurt me or lose me. I didn't want to hear him anymore. I begged him to leave my apartment and asked him to never look for me again. He stayed quiet; but all of a sudden when he stopped crying became aggressive. There was no doubt on my mind; that I didn't want anything to do with him. I told him I wanted to finish the contract lease. Then, Vincenzo became a violent man. He started to destroy everything that was in front of him and he pushed me against the wall. Like a lunatic he squeezed my face hard and threatened to sue me if I did not meet with the stipulated time in the contract. After articulating all kinds of insults, he slammed the door and left.

At that moment I knew I had an enemy. His love had turned to hatred and I had to think about things very well and with a cold heart a cold head, without putting any feeling in between, since my life could be in danger.

I called Maria Elena. She offered me her help.

--Come to my house; I will be waiting for you. Do it now right away! Tonight! --She told me.

I listened to her attentively. Half hour later, I was ready to leave. I ordered a taxi and ran to my friend's house.

María Elena welcomed me as if she were my own blood. I felt comforted to see her. I prepared a valerian tea that tasted wonderful. I told her the whole story without omitting details. She advised me prudence, also recommended not to forgive him under any circumstances.

—You have to change for another job so he won't find you so easy––She said, worried.

That night I could hardly sleep, I thought about my life as a disaster. It didn't count if I was pretty, prepared and smart, I realized I had bad luck in love, and I always ended up hurt. I tried to forget my nightmare, so I could go to work less depressed the next day.

When we arrived at the store, everyone seemed busy and even cheerful. No one suspected of my tragedy. While checking a merchandise, María Elena told me someone was calling me on the phone. I jumped around like a spring and went to answer immediately wondering who it could be. Maybe it was Vincenzo, though I refused to believe he dared to call me after everything that had happened.

However, I didn't hear anything, after a while, they hung up. My friend ran to where I was, eager to know, asked me if it was Vincenzo, I said I did not know, because they had hung up.

––I'm sure it was that bad guy, ––she said.

––If he you call you again, let me answer. I will send him to hell. Such a lunatic!

Ring, ring … again. My heart was pounding. María Elena went to answer quickly.

––*Pronto, pronto?* (Hello, hello) …

––*Pronto*, she suddenly heard on the phone; and immediately, she heard the voice of Vincenzo:

––Look, *bitch*! Tell the *whore* of your friend that I know she left the apartment without notice. She ran away from me! With whom has she gone this time? Tell me, *bitch*! Because you will also pay for being a *Pimp*. Warn Vera that I will go to her boss to tell her she is a drug trafficker and owes me money. Let's see if she doesn't throw her out. Are you listening to me, idiot?

––Do whatever you want, crazy *scum*. Now, you should listen to me: if you dare to bother her or hurt her, you will have to face me! She is not alone. Do you understand me!

Luck was on our side that day; my boss had gone out for coffee and didn't notice anything. The calls continued; but every time we answered, they hung up. After a few days, they no longer called, so I felt more confident.

*****

One night we left the store late because we had to take inventory. The streets were damp and dark, it had rained heavily and a light mist covered the city. We were walking along the cobblestone streets and having a pleasant conversation; suddenly, we felt that somebody was watching over us; when we turned around, we only saw a shadow reflected on the walls. We could not distinguish anything in particular. Though we got a little afraid.

We continued walking, and suddenly, I heard footsteps accompanied by the sound of the splash of the water accumulated on the sidewalk. At that instant, we lightened our pace; but the footsteps that we heard behind us also accelerated to the same pace. I turned around again, and I could see the silhouette of a man who seemed to wear a hat it covered part of his face.

––Maria Elena, hurry up! There is a man following us. I couldn't see clearly who he was, but I was sure he was pursuing us.

When Mary saw the guy, she thought about Vincenzo, but she still wasn't sure he was the man, because his hat did not allow to see his face clearly.

He noticed we had seen him and rapidly hid in an alley. María Elena told me she finally could see his face, and was almost sure, he was the maniac of Vincenzo.

––Hurry up, Vera! Walk fast, the man has left the alley
––She said, nervous.

Soon after, he approached us enough and I could detect he wanted to take out something of his jacket; perhaps, the weapon with which he intended to kill us. We were going to be attacked. God and the angels helped us, because at that moment a taxi passed; with a desperate gesture we asked him to stop. We onboard the car, quickly. Already inside the vehicle I felt I was short of breath and I saw María Elena was sweating profusely. We were nervous and confused. We thought, at one moment, what was happening was only product of our paranoia, and our imagination.

The taxi driver looked at us through the rearview mirror, and worried, asked us if we were okay. We tried to pretend that nothing happened, but the man did not believe us. He warned us that another taxi was coming, at high speed, behind us. María Elena turned to see, and the car was getting closer and closer to ours, to the point that it almost ran into the fender of the taxi in which we were going. The driver noticed and pulled roughly to stop. He ordered us to get off his taxi. When this happened the other car also stopped, making a thunderous shriek when braking. The man who got off the near taxi was Vincenzo. His expression was of hate and he looked stressed.

We ran fast towards the entrance of the subway station, stumbling upon everything we found in our path. Vincenzo did the same, he followed us.

Upon arriving at the ticket office window, our aggressor began to shout all kinds of insults, he was behaving like a maniac. In the midst of his madness he said he just wanted to talk. When he approached us, we saw that he put his hand inside his jacket pocket. María Elena turned pale and I suspected he was looking for the weapon. The man behind the ticket counter hid, everything was happening so fast but to me it seemed like an eternity. Two *carabinieri* peeked out, and whistle anxiously, and were running toward us. Their presence made Vincenzo give up his attempt, and as if nothing had happened, he returned where he had come from, without having had the opportunity to take out what he had in his pocket.

A moment later, we told the police that everything was in order. I remembered we were in the country illegally; denouncing Vincenzo would only bring us more problems. We arrived at the apartment exhausted, and trembling. Maria Elena and I went to the kitchen to have a drink, and she commented to me:

—I'm sure he wants to hurt us. He's been following us, who knows since when— said, almost unable to breathe. We have to be alert. Let's go to sleep, tomorrow will be another day and we will have our minds in a better condition as to think well. Good night, Vera. May God protect us! —She added nervously.

In the morning the phone rang, when I answered, a man's voice told me:

—Hello, my dear Vera. How could you do this to me?

I paralyzed when I realized it was Vincenzo, I did not know what to do, so I replied:

—It's a wrong number.

Then, with a dark voice, he added:

—I know it's you, Vera. You, *cheap bitch*! You will regret it, now I know where you are. I will come for both of you and cut off your necks. *Damn bitches*!

María Elena was taking a shower. I interrupted her to tell her that Vincenzo already knew I was with her and he had threatened to kill us. She left the bathroom in a hurry. Her eyes widened open as if she had seen a phantom, she could not hide her terror. After, she hurriedly went to check the locks. I asked her to calm down. She responded by asking me:

—Vera, have you realized we cannot even notify the police?! We do not have work permits and we are illegal immigrants. We must think very well what to do.

The next day, we woke up in fear, but life had to continue. We went to work as usual, and before arriving, we passed by a bar to drink an *expresso;* when we entered, Vincenzo was there. Apparently, Rome was not that big. I considered it a chance or maybe a bad turn of fate. After the surprise, we ran nonstop until we reached the train station.

Vincenzo was like the shadow of evil. It appeared when we least expected it. It was dangerous, because he already knew our routine and also the address in which we were living. María Elena told me he was going crazy and could kill us. I didn't think he was capable of that, but we couldn't take the risk.

A few weeks passed and we had some peace of mind. The phone no longer rang and everything went back to normal; however, the bad news didn't wait too much. My boss called me, said she wanted to talk to me about something very delicate.

––Vera, I need to tell you that you can't continue working here. Yesterday afternoon, when I was closing the store, a man named Vincenzo Andreotti approached me, to say he was the proprietor of the apartment in which you live, and you had left this apartment without complying with the contract you signed.

When she mentioned his name, I feared the worse.

––That man has denounced you to the authorities and we will both be in a big problem for that. I can go to jail for hiring an illegal. You can be deported, etcetera.

––But … madam … Please allow me to tell you my version of that story.

–I am sure you won't lie to me, but you must understand we are both in a mess.

—I imagine, that the authorities must have all your data already. Vera you must leave this city before it's too late, ––she pleaded.

I returned immediately to the apartment. I called the travel agency and bought a ticket to Guatemala. This time, there would be no return.

When the time for my departure came, María Elena was drowned into tears. She had supported me so much time; she had been a good friend. To say goodbye caused us great sadness. I didn't know if I would see her again.

*****

When I arrived at the airport, I saw policemen running from side to side, it seemed they were following or looking for someone; I thought it was me so I panicked.

I went to the bathroom to hide while waiting for

the call to get on board. When I got out of the bathroom, I saw them moving around again, it stressed me even more. I refused to believe that, because of a sick jealous man I could go to jail. Already inside the plane I felt better. I was more relaxed; but my thoughts were interrupted when I saw again the *carabinieri* inside the plane looking for that someone that I expected not to be me.

When they passed by my side, one of them asked for my passport, scrutinizing every page of it, looking at my photo, with a suspicious glance, then returned it to me, without saying a word. They did the same with a couple of other passengers and left without saying anything. I was in shock; my forehead was pearled by the sweat. Finally, they closed the door of the plane and I began to cry uncontrollably. Through the window I saw the dome of the Vatican and thought to myself that in that beautiful city I had left my illusions and my failed hopes of starting a new life. Everything was lost. I was broke, because I didn't have any penny in my bag. But returning to Guatemala would guarantee my freedom and peace of mind.

SECOND PART

"All the battles in life serve to teach us something,
including those we lose."
Pablo Cohelo

The flight became eternal and my uncertainty grew as the hours passed, I did not know what I would find on my return. I wondered how I would tell my parents my story. Also, what would I do with my life when I arrived in Guatemala.

Everything became a giant uncertainty to me. To have left Italy had been the best decision for me? Again, and again I was torturing myself with those questions and my mind was getting tired. I gave a paused to my insecurities and closed my eyes until I woke up with the voice of the pilot announcing slight turbulence, we were almost arriving in Guatemala. I had slept many hours, thanks to a sleeping pill Maria Elena had given me before leaving.

The bad memories with Vincenzo in that city passed through my head, as if it were a horror movie; It hurt me to think my failure was due to a crazy, sick man. It was clear my luck did not revolve around love. At that moment it didn't make any difference anymore, I was on my way home and I was sure that my life would take another course.

The captain announced we would land soon. My heart was pounding and I became restless. I was exhausted and my legs hurt from being seated for so many hours. I got tired trying to understand why I had allowed that man to have made me suffer so much in the attempt to improve my sentimental life. In the end, I concluded that happiness was not for everyone. At least, it wasn't for me.

*****

As soon as I arrived at customs and heard my people accent, I vibrated with excitement, because I realized I was already in my land. The people´s joy with their sales on the streets, and the natives with their beautiful colorful costumes, confirmed me that returning to Guatemala had been the best decision. However, I had mixed feelings. The desire to cry invaded me; I didn't know if it was of happiness or of the sadness caused by my failure.

From a distance, I noticed my parents were coming to receive me. When I saw my mother, I couldn't contain my tears; she hugged me, comforted me with affectionate words, and gave me a strong and prolonged welcome kiss. Dad did the same, he squeezed me tight. Then, we got into the car and headed home.

During the journey, I watched in amazed at the faces of the people. Their friendly expressions always had a smile to show everybody. Their toasted skin color and its native features portraited in time the history of our ancestors, who remained anchored in the 18th century in its volcanoes, in its elegant and imposing colonial mansions, also in its monasteries and churches. A true treasure for the history of humanity.

On the walls of the houses hung bougainvillea's waterfalls of different colors. Its cobbled streets smell like coffee, freshly made *tortillas*, hot chocolate and all those *delicacies* which had Guatemalan *cuisine*.

From the moment we entered in Antigua, I noticed that my city was more beautiful and charming than ever. The weather was ideal; a cool breeze blew and accompanied us as we headed home. We didn't stop talking during the journey. Mom never mentioned or asked why I came back; it was very wise on her part; it would have been very hard for me to tell her everything it had happened.

My father drove the car into the garage. When we crossed the threshold of the door, I was delighted with the particular aroma that came from the kitchen. A melancholically joy enveloped me, mixed with a little guilt for having left my family in trying to pursue a dream which became a nightmare; however, that did not matter to me anymore. I was already with the people who loved me unconditionally and with whom I felt safe.

There was Dalila, whom I love very much. She is the woman who helps my mother in the house. She comes from Santa María de Jesús, a small town near Antigua, Dalila is always wearing a *huipil* a native skirt embroidered in colorful flowers, and in her head a cloth crown in bright colors.

—Miss Vera, welcome back! —She said with a sincere smile and her firm indigenous accent.

—Hello, Dalila. I feel like it was yesterday that I left *Antigua*. It's good to be home, —I said, not still believing, I was already there.

There was, also, a boy in his twenties from Atitlan, where the great mystical lake is located. He was always willing to work at anything to provide for himself and his family; that is why my mother had given him work to alleviate the poverty his family suffered. As I passed my bedroom, I stood at the doorstep, for some time, until I realized that I was back home. The window in my bedroom overlooked the street and was protected by wrought iron bars and flower pots of various colors were placed at the base. I put my dresses in the old wooden closet. The bed still had that blanket made of bright colored yarn, which infused energy and a certain spirituality.

Sitting on my bed, I remembered when my parents, many years ago, had bought the house from a man who left for the United States in pursuit of the *American dream*.

When I was little, I loved being in the courtyard that was near a stone fountain, visited by birds, who drank water, and whom I used to chase to catch them, without ever accomplished it. All bedrooms, living room and dining room were around the central courtyard. The house was old and kept the colonial architecture, so typical of the place and of that epoch. Nothing had changed, except me, who had a bag of disappointments and sorrows I carried.

That night, I understood I needed to go to *Las Mercedes* cathedral to see if God helped me find my way. I set it on my agenda for the next day. I lay on my bed and extended my arms and legs to take off the numbness that I still felt after that long journey. Then I went to the bathroom, took a shower and dressed for the welcome dinner.

Dalila had prepared a splendid meal. Some friends of my parents and my best friend Rosa arrived, she was a faithful companion I had in college when I was studying journalism; also, someone who could not miss: Father Sánchez, the parish priest of the church.

Eating again in clay dishes decorated with *Mayan* figures confirmed me that I was home. The food placed on the wooden table were *hilachas, enchiladas, bananas in mole* and *yuca* with *chicharron*, which were the pork fried fat strips. in addition to other typical dishes; It was a feast. Dalila had done a marvelous job. I missed that meal so much.

We sat at the table and before cheering the palate, we thanked God for the food. My parents were devoted Catholics and they raised me in the faith; in addition, with the priest sitting at the head of the table, prayer was essential.

During dinner questions arose; Rosa asked the first.

——Vera, tell me, how did it go in Italy? Why did you come back? Why did you do this? Why did you do that? Why...? The others seconded her with the interrogation, without any bad intentions.

——We thought you would be living in Rome, added Father Sanchez, after taking a sip of wine.

——Yes. The truth is that ... well, it is ... I wanted to stay, but the papers did not come out and I could not be illegal, it was a risk to be arrested and deported. It was better for me, to get out on my own free will, I said, very naturally.

——The important thing is that you have returned and you are with us again, ——Mom said, not wanting to know anything else.

Dad pointed out the same and told them they were happy I was back. In order not to give them more to think about. I told them my experiences as a tourist, the wonderful places I saw and the close friendship I had with María Elena, my Honduran friend. With that last comment, the conversation about my stay in Italy ended.

My father, wisely, redirected the talk towards political issue and the night ended pleasantly. Rosa, before leaving, said, she would call me to go for coffee at a new place they had opened, giggling she said, it was filled with foreign guys who came to *Antigua* to take Spanish classes. I thought it was great to go out there to have fun with my friend, and also, to remember old times.

After the other guests left, I said goodnight to my parents, and went to my room; there I felt a great inner peace, and as soon as I put my head on the pillow, I fell asleep deeply.

It was a new day and a new dawn; I was far from problems and threats. I got up with the song of the birds and the hustle caused by the arrival of the baker in his bicycle, who carried the delicious and freshly baked bread to the door. Dalila made me scrambled eggs, for breakfast, with tomato and onion, then, she put bread on the table with a steaming cup of coffee.

Everything was so different. Life was more natural, less complicated, without lies or artifice. Then I went for a walk, and saw around me, everything more beautiful than before: the landscapes, its nature, the greenery was everywhere and the flowers were always adorning the gardens, walls and the base of the windows. I did not understand how could I pretend to find a new life in a culture that was very different from mine. But, unfortunately, I had learned the bad way. Everything it happened to me made me reflect and recognize that between fantasy and truth there is a great abyss. I felt that there was nothing better than being in my own country, in my house, with the ones I loved.

Walking through narrow and cobbled streets, I arrived at the cathedral and met Father Sánchez, who greeted me with a big smile. Then, I asked him to confess me.

During confession I revealed him that I hated my-self for being so stupid and for believing that everyone was good. I confided him, that for the first time, I had felt a deep hatred for a man and, powerlessly, I burst into a sea of tears, I had held for so long.

Father Sánchez had known me since I was a little girl, he approached me, put his hand on my shoulder and looked at me as if he knew my pain; He comforted me with great love and advised me to trust in God, he said, he would take care of putting me on the right path.

After I'd done my penance, which I thought I deserved for being so innocent, I came home. I felt as if I had been born again; to have clean my soul of rancor and bitterness, through forgiveness, brightened my day.

Mom was very happy when she knew I was coming from the church. I continued to feel calm because she still wouldn't ask anything about my unexpected return; however, mothers intuit what's wrong with their children, they have a sixth sense; and without needing to tell her, she knew my heart had been broken and that things hadn't gone well for me in Italy. I had noticed it in her gaze, and in the way, she hugged me when she came for me at the airport.

******

The days went by quickly. I went to look for work to have something to do, and to help me forget. I decided to go to the local newspaper to see if I collaborated writing about the tourist places of my country and my city; it was a subject that fascinated me and that I could do.

Antigua was declared in 1979, *Cultural Heritage of Humanity* by UNESCO; for that reason, and because of the legacy left by the *Mayan* civilization, it was a very attractive place for tourists; therefore, there were too many stories to tell and spread throughout the world.

I made an appointment for an interview in the local newspaper hoping to get lucky. I arrived early in the morning and, Mr. Rómulo Castaneda, manager of the *El País* newspaper, was waiting for me. As soon as I entered his office, he immediately, interviewed me. The newspaper headquarters were located in an old colonial style building, like almost everything there. His office was spacious, bright and had some furniture in leather that looked very old.

As soon as I sat down, I handed him my summary. He looked at it thoughtfully and read it carefully. When he finished, he found it interesting that I had lived in Rome, he said that people who traveled and had the opportunity to live in other cities got a better mental opening than those who had never left their borders.

I felt happy for his appreciation and just hoped he wouldn't ask me for the reason of my departure and less of my return; They were situations I considered private, and for which I would have to lie flatly. The interview was brief, and to the point. As soon as it was over, he said he would call me.

That night I was going to see Rosa, and I was excited to go out and have a little fun. Several weeks had passed and I felt more stable and confident in my land.

I never stopped communicating with my savior and hero Maria Elena, in part, I owed her my life; and although, I missed her a lot the conditions were not good to pay her a visit. I was sure that one day we would meet again.

The last time we talked, she told me, Vincenzo had called her to apologize for behaving so badly; and said, he loved me and his jealousy had driven him to madness. She had talked to him, as if nothing happened, because she didn't want to have him as an enemy. In addition, she said to him that I was far away, and she didn't know where. That made Vincenzo not to call her again.

I knew that if I wanted to go to visit my friend one day, it could not be soon, I had to let some prudent time pass, to not expose her. And on my part, I still had the fear of meeting with that demon.

I confess, I was hoping that if I ever return to Rome, he would be married and have a family made up of ten children, so, he wouldn't harass me anymore.

In my worst nightmares I would see him chasing me with a knife in his hand to kill me and, just as he would approach, I would wake up in a jump breathing agitatedly and sweating in terror. The recurrence of those nightmares made me realize that the shadow of that man was still chasing me and that I was traumatized.

*****

We arrived at a place, which was on fashion, called *Maya* Bar. It was packed with people; about to explode. It was a very nice, bohemian site, full of young foreigners. It was a colonial-style house with the traditional courtyard and a fountain made of colorful mosaics in the middle. In the hallways there were small tables with brightly colored checkered tablecloths and red candles in the center. A particular scent of incense was breathed in every corner of the place. The atmosphere was relaxed and cheerful at the same time. The bar was full of people chatting amicably; many of them spoke in: English, German or French. There were also quite a few North Americans.

We sat at a table for four and asked for tequila. After two *per capita,* Rosa and I were already laughing out loud and fixing the world. It was incredible the feeling of freedom that I sheltered. My expression had changed, now, I felt in peace, I was full of energy and I sparkled.

From one moment to another a girl approached us to offered us her divination services through the Tarot cards, we did not know whether to believe it or not, but it was another way of having fun and spending time; for the night was just beginning.

The fortune teller looked like a gypsy woman, she wore a wide skirt and on her head she had a turban with little lights of various colors that looked so funny, like an ambulatory Christmas tree, so, we had to hide our laughter, so as not to offend her ; also, we didn't want her to tell us bad things.

——Good evening girls. Do you want to know your future? ——She asked enthusiastically, while her turban shone through the flashing lights.

——What do you say, Rosa? ——I asked my friend.

——Yes. It's fine for me, ——she replied without thinking it for a second.

The clairvoyant sat in front of us and started with me. I hoped she wouldn't tell me something ugly, I had already expiated for my sins, and at the moment, I just wanted to hear positive things. She spread her cards on the table, stood thoughtful and watching, attentively, the cards, said:

——You have suffered a lot. The Tarot cards are saying you have been looking for love in the wrong place. I see, here, two people who are very happy to be with you;

but I also see you alone and crying a lot. Someone, who is far away, misses you and wants to be with you, but does not know how to do it. That person, who can be a man, is suffering and wandering as a soul in sorrow. He is not good for you, for he can be your downfall, besides, he looks dangerous——she emphasized. Then she continued:

——The cards, also, say that you will enjoy a great event. A person who is not from here will appear into your life; he doesn't have to do with your past, to the contrary, he will come to light up your life. Everything would be *ok* if you don't make any more mistakes. You cannot complain. The cards predict everything positive for you,——she added.

I listened to her without blinking. I felt already positive since I was away from that nightmare called Vincenzo, and I liked what she was saying.

——But, beware! I see danger. You are going to make long trips full of challenges. The cards announce that you will be accompanied by a man who will play an important role in your life. Oh my God! It will be an adventure!——she said with excitement.

——I interrupted her to ask:

——Is that man from here?——whishing it wasn't Vincenzo.

——I don't see it clearly, but he seems to be from this part of the world.

——And in relation to my work, what do you see?

——I see everything positive about it. In general, you will meet many interesting people and you will enter in a mysterious world you've never imagined.

——The storm has passed. Now the rainbow will rise up for you. You must not see the past, it is black and confusing. Always walk forward.

When she finished, she approached me, stroked my head gently and looked at me with an expression of pity; she ended up telling me:

——You have really suffered tons, my girl!

It was Rosa's turn. She opened her eyes widely, a little scared. The gypsy, with a loud laugh, advised her not to be scared too soon.

——For you, miss, everything is accomplished. I don't see anything strange or bad in your future; I 'm sorry to tell you it's a little less interesting than your friend's. However, life will reward you with a love, a good man, who speaks another language. —Rosa, unconsciously, saw the boys at the bar again. I laughed at her; she was so naïve.

——I see a wedding, ——she continued, ——and half a dozen children giving you a pleasant trouble. There is nothing else.

Rosa felt a little disenchanted with what the woman had said. She wanted to travel, leave her land, have new experiences; but it was written she would stay in Guatemala, she would become a dedicated wife, and a typical mother. She would have a normal life, and to some extent, monotonous and boring.

——Well, not bad, friend, ——I said, ——you will be very happy. It was what I would have liked to hear for me. I would have been pleased if she told me that I would find my prince charming. But, apparently, fate has some challenges for me. I don't know if I like better what it holds for you.

Then, we toast with another tequila wishing the best for both of us. After the toast, Rosa told me:

——Friend, you'll be famous. I hope you remember me when you succeed, ——she said, laughing out loud.

The night was going well and we were having a lot of fun. I saw my watch and was alarmed by the hour; it was late and we had to go back. I felt a little dizzy from the *tequilas* and Rosa´s eyes were red and she had a weird gaze, but we still felt kind of normal.

Before leaving, I got up to go to the bathroom, and as I was walking through that swarm of people, I suddenly, stumbled into the shoe of a man who grabbed me by the arm just as I was about to fall on a table. I thought the *tequilas* were doing the unwanted effect.

The one who rescued me had saved me from doing a scene, although, he said that he was sorry, he offered me a thousand apologies and introduced himself as Charif Fernández Abosaid.

As soon as I saw him, I liked him, he was a handsome man, his features were not Latin, but rather Arab, his eyes were large, dark green, with thick and big eyelashes. The skin was white and had abundant hair; too long, to my taste.

—My name is Vera Gomez. I am Guatemalan, ——I said proudly, straightening my dress and wiping with my hands the remaining traces of the *guacamole* on my dress.

——What a shame with you, Vera! Luckily you didn't fall on top of those guys. I managed to grab you in time, ——he said with a frank smile. That's why I would like to invite you for a drink, let me do something, so it would be easier for you to forgive me.

——I am with a friend. Our table is the one at the end of the hall. If you want to sit with us, you are welcome. Even though, we are almost leaving.

——I will be delighted to chat with you, even for a moment.

When he reached the table, he sat down and Rosa

looked surprised. Then he called the waiter and offered us something to drink. Rosa, without thinking too much, asked for another *tequila*, so he ordered another round. Rosa started laughing; the *tequilas* were, already, doing their thing. To me, on the contrary, the drunken signs left at once, when I was about to land on that table and cause a little chaos in the place.

—What do you do, girls? —asked, Charif.

—I'm trying to get a job as a journalist in the local newspaper, *El País*, —I replied.

—I, help my parents in a *souvenir* shop near the *Santo Domingo* hotel. —Rosa said,

—Where do you come from, Charif? — I asked.

—I am from Colombia. I teach Spanish to foreigners in an academy. I have been here for four months and I love the place, and above all, my work. I have about ten students from all over the world.

—Wonderful, —I said, — therefore, you must know many foreigners; I want to write an article about tourism in *Antigua,* and it might be interesting to talk, also, about the Spanish schools.

—Good thing we have something in common, —Charif said excited. If you need any information do not hesitate to call me, here is my card.

I could only give him my phone number written on a paper napkin. Rosa gave him the one of the *souvenir* shops. We left all three at the same time. On the street, we said goodbye as if we were not going to see each other again.

—Rose, can we get home walking or should we ask for a taxi? I feel very dizzy, —I said.

She laughed without stopping, like a lunatic. A taxi passed; We did all kinds of gestures for it to stop and save us from walking home in that state. Finally, we entered the car. Upon arriving home, I just wished I had no hangover the next day.

I woke up well, and to the sound of the baker's bicycle horn. I heard the phone was ringing insistently. I ran to answer. It was Mr. Castaneda who wanted to see me at around eleven.

I arrived very punctual to the newspaper. I entered the office of which, hopefully, would be my boss; As soon as he saw me, he invited me to come in and feel comfortable. After a few minutes he offered me a cup of coffee, and without speaking much, told me I had been accepted to work in the tourism sector of the newspaper. With a fraternal smile he welcomed me to his team. I left the newspaper as if I had won the lottery. I stood in front of the building and took a deep breath of satisfaction, some tears, out of happiness, escaped from my eyes.

I was excited to work on something I liked to do. As soon as I got home, I told my parents, they reacted well and were happy. I felt whole. I had the people I loved the most in life, a job, an old friend with whom I had seas of fun, I was in my land. Ah...! and also, I had a new friend: Charif Fernández Abosaid.

*****

My first day of work, was focused on meeting all the newspaper staff. They told me what my cubicle would be and the computer I would work with, which by the way, was a bit old-fashioned, but it still worked. On top of my desk there was a camera, an essential tool for the work I would develop. The building, like every other in the city, was not modern, but it had all the comforts and preserved the colonial architecture of *Antigua*.

As soon as I took possession of my tiny office, I started looking for updated information on tourism in Guatemala. I was pleased that I was going to do a field job and I wouldn't spend the whole day inside my cubicle. It was about visiting the most important historic places in the country, taking photographs and writing attractive information for the brochures that would stimulate the entire world to visit Guatemala, among other activities that could come.

In the office I met a very nice girl named Xiomara, she would assist me in my work. The first time I saw her I found her very active and pleasant, besides, collaborating.

Every day I woke up very early to go running, to do some exercise. My eyes were delighted to see the majestic *Hunahpú* volcano, which stood in front of the town, vigilant and silent. Its name comes from the *Maya-Quiché* language. It's one of the semi-gods, the twins, whose story in narrated in the *Popol Vuh.*

Then I go somewhere to have breakfast or just to have a coffee. That was my routine before I go to work. Sometimes Rosa accompanied me. When we were walking, we talked about the present without ever mentioning the past which no longer existed for me; it had stayed away, hidden in some cave, and I didn't want it to come back. My life now had other shades; I had grown in every sense of the word and I was happy with my work and everything else around me.

There was a lot to do in the newspaper. The dates of *Holy Week* and other important celebrations were, for me, work and not fun. The world had to know what happened in a city with so much history and tradition, in those days.

We produce audiovisual material of the festivities celebrated in the city; also, everything related to the Spanish teaching academies in *Antigua,* which can be attractive to so many foreigners. The director had entrusted me to make some brochures on this topic, and at that moment, my friend Charif appeared in my mind.

I called him and asked for an interview. He seemed happy to hear my voice again, and he said it would be a pleasure to answer all my questions. He invited me to lunch at a nice restaurant to discuss the issue. That afternoon I wanted to look pretty so I worked hard to be irresistible. Recently they had opened a shop, where I went to buy a beige sweater and some tight jeans, which would show my *derriere* stand out in a suggestive way. My hair had already grown, it was below my shoulders, falling like a wild black waterfall. I had realized I had gone back to my old image of a genuine *Guatemalan* girl.

Upon entering the restaurant, I could see Charif sitting at the bar having a beer. He looked terribly attractive; he was wearing a white linen shirt and gray pants, I thought, he was too elegant for the occasion. When I approached, he greeted me with some distance, I thought he was reacting shyly because we didn't know each other so well.

We sat next to the fountain which was adorned by tropical flowers, around it. When I saw all those colors in nature, I realized that I would always be surrounded by beauty.

I regretted, again, having left Guatemala to pursue an absurd dream of which I was grateful to have woken up.

—What do you want to drink Vera? I hope it's not *tequila,*—he joked.

——I feel like drinking a cold beer. Only one, because I have to go back to my office.

——It looks I will drink the same. It's a bit hot this morning, out of the ordinary.

A few minutes later, we were getting into the subject. He told me about his experiences as a teacher at the Spanish academy, he said he felt honored to be teaching his language.

—To begin with, my dear Vera, the place is called *Academia de Español Quiché* and we are eager to teach to all who want to come to Antigua, to learn the Spanish language. The place is located at Octava calle poniente, number 6. I am professor Fernández, and my students love me, also: I'm single, —— said jokingly. Before I begin to tell you my whole story, I have something to add: *you look beautiful and I want to keep seeing you.*

——This is a serious interview, Charif, ——I said with a slightly mischievous smile; However, I accept your compliments. Could we start? ——I asked with a little coquetry.

——I'm all ears, Vera. Go ahead, and excuse my sense of humor.

——Don't apologize, I find it very nice to work in that way.

The waiter brought us the beers, and some *chorizo* and *tortilla* as snacks, courtesy of the house.

Charif said his passion for teaching had its roots in Bogotá, Colombia, where he was born on a cold and wet morning in 1948.

——Literature has always captivated me since I was little, my father was a devoted reader, my mother is of Lebanese origin, and dedicated herself to raise us and to be a nice housewife, ——he said with great pride.

—During my adolescence, I read a lot and wrote some poems, short stories, and other texts, which I still keep in my father's office. Unfortunately, he already died. I have been passionate about traveling and when I learned about this work, I applied. Now I am happy to be here.

With little humility, he added:

—I'm nice, communicative, flexible and I have a lot of patience and I wish for my students to learn Spanish well. It seems to me that being a teacher in another country enriches you and gives you the opportunity to meet many people, share experiences and be updated on what is happening in the world. I have felt very sympathetic to my students of *Antigua*, I am almost like a priest and a psychologist to all of them. It is a profession that makes my life to have a purpose because I love helping others.

I listened very carefully. When he finished his speech, I didn't know what else to ask him; he had told me about his virtues, his motivations and his experiences in a summarized way.

——How many students do you have and where do most of them come from?——I asked.

——Well, Vera, the number varies depending on the time of year. I have between ten and twenty students; most of them come from Europe. Those who come least are those from the United States. Overall, I have noticed that they love Guatemalan culture and food; In addition, some return to their country with a girlfriend, and sometimes, even married. When we talk, they say that Latin women are charming and affectionate.

The guys practice all kinds of sports, including, climbing the volcano; they also, like to go to the bohemian bars of *Antigua*. That interaction helps them to learn the language very quickly. I am very happy with my work and even more after meeting you. ——He said, winking an eye.

——And the facilities, Charif, do you think they are adequate?

——Yes, of course, they are. The classrooms are large, ventilated and full of light; in addition to that, all apprentices receive the necessary material to advance on their studies. There is also a cafeteria inside the academy where they sell Guatemalan food, such as *tamales*, which are delicious, by the way. Students like to sit in the hallway that is in front of the courtyard, where they enjoy a lot of greenery. They love the spring weather that always prevails in *Antigua*. In my opinion, you couldn't ask for more.

—I would like to take some pictures of the facilities and the students. We are going to take out a brochure to promote the academies in England, specially, the one, in which you work; if the principal agrees, of course.

——I don't think there is any problem," he said. After lunch and coffee, we can go to the principal's office.

The waiter brought us a delicious *carne asada* (charcoal meat) with fried beans, bananas, *tortillas* and *guacamole*, which we began to eat anxiously. I was hungry and I noticed that Charif was too. Now, Vera, it's your turn ——he told me.

——My turn for what?

——Now, you have to tell me a little about your life.

At that moment, I felt worried. What would I tell him? That in addition to study journalism in my city, I went out one day to Italy with the purpose of forgetting my failure in love and got almost killed and put inside of an Italian jail. I couldn't tell him that horrible episode of my life. I would have to lie.

—Look, Charif, my life has been uninteresting. My mother said I was born the day when the volcano was active, on February 11, 1955. I remember my childhood with great joy, my parents have always loved each other, and without being a millionaire, I had all the comforts.

I, on my part, studied at a nun school here and graduated with average grades. Then I went to university to study journalism. That is all; what else could I tell you. Well, that at the present, I am in the newspaper *El País* working with Mr. Castaneda, who is my boss; I, also, have an intimate friend named Rosa, the girl you met that night with some extra *tequilas*.

—How great! I loved your brief description —he told me. A lifetime in four lines; It shows that you know how to write.

We were ready to order dessert; but we chose to better go to the cafeteria of the academy, and then talk to the director.

The afternoon went by quickly and I returned to my office with everything I needed as to make the brochure, and with more curiosity to learn more about Charif's life.

I had never been to Colombia and I would have liked him to tell me something about his land.

I returned to my house a little tired. Mom told me that Dalila had my dinner ready. I went to the kitchen, I ate a little, I was still bursting after that meal with Charif. To keep Dalila from feeling offended, I told her that I've had a big lunch at the office, and that I didn't feel very well in my stomach. I went straight to my room and fell asleep, thinking about how interesting was that man with Arab features.

*****

The following days passed without news. I visited local events and parties, and prepared the reports asked by my boss.

One day very early, the phone rang, it was Charif.

——Good morning, Vera. How are you doing this morning? Do you know that you are still in my mind? So, I would like to see you again, ——he said in a melodious voice.

I liked that awakening; it seemed that things were going better for me. I told him I would be delighted, and agreed to meet with him in the same bar in which we had first met. Nevertheless; fear arose in me, a ghost of the past was still haunting me, and its name was: *Vincenzo.*

It was cold that night. I dressed accordingly to go out. I arrived at eight o'clock. There was Charif with my *sweater* in his hand.

——You left it forgotten the other day, ——he said.

I smiled and thanked him. He looked very handsome. He wore a leather jacket and his green eyes had the sparkle of emeralds. He was happy and willing to have a good time.

We sat at a table at the end of the hall so that the activity of the other guests would not bother us. It was not a job interview, but a date that could become a romance, perhaps.

Charif was charming and flattering. I felt pleased. He asked me about the brochures, coincidentally I had the sample of one of them in my bag, I showed it to him and he liked it. Then we ignored everything related to work and dedicated to talk about us, to know more about our lives.

After a couple of *tequilas*, I talked more and dared to tell him what had happened to me in Italy. I didn't want to have secrets with someone who was becoming so special to me. I liked him and I knew he liked me too; there was no doubt about that.

When he heard my story, he felt sorry for me, he said that I did not deserve that someone so mean had crossed my path. Then, he approached me, and as a demonstration of affection, stroked my cheek with his hand and his fingers brushed my lips very gently. I felt a slight chill running down my spine.

Having told him my story helped me to let off steam. Ejecting all the pain I kept inside of me was therapeutic, I wanted to begin a romance, or a friendship, without lies or secrets.

After my story, he took my hands and looking into my eyes he confessed to me he liked me. I did not know what to say. My face lit up and without saying a word on my part, he understood he was reciprocated.

The waiter approached with the menu; which forced us to take a pause on our talk. Once we ordered the food, I wanted to know more about him.

—Tell me, Charif, how is your land and how was your life in Colombia? I asked with a lot of curiosity.

He began to tell his story:

—Well, as you know, I was born in Bogotá. I have three sisters. My mother has been a widow for many years. I miss them all,—he said, sighing.

—I studied literature at the university and graduated with honors.

——You, see? I was a good guy, ——he said jokingly. Then, continued:

——My maternal grandparents were Lebanese and my paternal grandparents were Colombian. Those of Lebanese origin made a whole tour from Lebanon to finish settling in Bogotá. Those were difficult years for them and an adventure to come from so far away. I admired them a lot. I grew up with them, in addition to my parents.

——I feel very proud of my Lebanese blood, of my roots ——he added——, breathing profoundly. My father was a true Colombian man, he was born in *Tolima*, a region that is located in the center-west of the country; and my mother, although, she was born in Cuba, was more Lebanese than her parents. My sisters are from Bogotá.

I am the *last Lebanese* in my family, that makes me proud, because the culture of my ancestors is rich in traditions and one of the oldest in the world. At the same time, it saddens me not to preserve this tradition in my family, for with time, it will be lost.

I know how to cook their food thanks to my grandmother Maria who taught me. I remember, when I was little, she would sit me in a high stool to explain to me, in a Spanish with a strong Arabic accent, how to cook dishes such as *tabbouleh, baba ghanoush, kibbe, falafel, baklava* and many other recipes.

——Someday, I want to cook for you Lebanese food. I'm an expert, ——he said proudly.

——Are you serious? ——I asked. I would be very pleased to try that exotic food. Yes, I accept, ——I said laughing, without even knowing the day of the invitation.

Charif continued:

—Of my generation, I am the first Colombian and I am the *last Lebanese,* since I am the oldest in my family. My paternal grandmother, Celina, widowed when my father was six years old. Grandfather Rafael, her husband, was an important landowner in the Tolima region, he had two sisters. Those were difficult times for they died of yellow fever, almost at the same time, my grandfather died of a cerebral hemorrhage, before turning thirty. My father was alone. Over the years he was responsible for the care of grandma Celina.

They inherited my grandfather's land; but since grandma Celina had no idea how to manage that inheritance, her family seeing her distraught and confused, offered to help her; nevertheless, greed and bad intention seized their relatives who, using tricks and lies, stole her land.

They were almost left on the street, so he had no choice but to go to the city of Bogotá, to find sustenance for her and my father. That made my father hated his mother's family and not to see them again. Over the years, those infamous sought him for help after they had stripped them of their property. That's why if you ask me about these thieves, I don't know much about them, although I met them, I wouldn't want to see them again, ——he said a little annoyed.

——That awful! Poor of your grandmother. She must have felt betrayed and totally abandoned — I intervened.

——She, to shovel her grief, took refuge in God and in her work. She had to educate my father and give him all he needed. The problem was that she became a fanatic of religion and when I had to go to school, she pressured

Dad to enroll me in a Catholic one. I was barely seven years old. I could never adapt to those practices nor did I understand the priests. I exaggerate if I say I was there for more than six months.

One day I ran away from school because a clergyman wanted to punish me with violence and to lock me in a room. Don't be scared, but I grabbed him by an arm, kicked him on his leg and ran away, crossed the soccer field, jumped the fence of the school and came to my house. I didn't have to walk much, since it was close. There, my Catholic life ended.

—Poor! I understand you, Charif, although I believe in my religion, those things should never happen. Fanaticism leads to breaking the rules of respect and becomes almost a disease —I said.

—Returning to my father's story, to pay for his studies, he had to study during the day and work at night. After that double effort, one day he graduated as a business administrator. It was not easy for him to tolerate my grandmother Celina, who due to what she had suffered had become a bitter and despotic person.

Charif remembered with tears that his father's greatest ambition had been to be a physician:

—In that search, one day, my father won a scholarship to study ophthalmology at a prestigious university in the United States, but my grandmother Celina did not want him to leave because she did not want to be alone. She had become an abusive person and displayed her bitterness by repressing him of everything. That exacerbation by religion made my father run away from religious practices; therefore, that time I escaped from school, he understood me and did not punish me.

—When you were without a school, what did

your father do? He must have been very upset, even if he wasn't a practitioner, I guessed.

—All the contrary. I felt that he rewarded me by enrolling me in a school that was secular and had very little to do with priests. In that atmosphere I spent part of my childhood and adolescence. It was a Swiss school, there I learned two languages: French and Italian. At first, there were some marked differences with the school chaplain, because of the bad experiences I had during my childhood, but, over time, he was one of the few religious I accepted in my life. It was different and mundane, like all human beings. Later I learned that he became a cardinal in Rome and it sounded like a possible pope candidate.

—Charif, what an interesting story; go on, please, —I motivated him.

——My father was a strict and a cold person. He did not know how to express his love due to the lack of affection in his childhood.

Although he was always indifferent to me, he gave me everything I asked for, including my own apartment inside the house. It always made me feel independent and somehow consented me.

My mother is a homely and submissive woman. She was always watching over Dad. As a young woman she was very beautiful, she still is; she has brown hair, huge eyes with large eyelashes and a fleshy mouth.

It is important to tell you that *Mom* has always been an enigmatic person. Since adolescence he developed a special capacity that some consider extra sensorial: she has the gift of predicting tragic events.

It impressed to those whom she told the story about a black Virgin who appeared to her to let her know the misfortunes that were going to happen; above all, those related to air accidents; But one day, she felt alarmed about it and asked to the black Virgin to please tell her nothing about what was going to happen.

I inherited some of his gifts, although differently. In a moment of my adolescence I immersed myself in the literature that had to do with paranormal phenomena.

Charif's story, no doubt, was getting interesting; Unfortunately, the waiter approached to offer us dessert and Charif had to pause.

—And then, —I said, anxiously.

—Since I wanted to know what made me different from the others; I began to experiment with my *psyche* and my mind, and that is how I came to have experiences of astral unfolding in which I connected with a being that I could never identify, but it guided me during the trips.

During that period, I realized that I could move objects without touching them; that phenomenon is known as telekinesis. This happened to me when I was very angry or anxious.

Finally, after researching, through reading and receiving psychological help, I discovered, that my ability was in my hands, they were an instrument of healing and relief. I had several experiences, especially when it came to children.

I remember once, in a small town in Boyacá, I entered a grocery store, there was a little boy who was crying as he rubbed his hand. It seemed that something had happened to him and he could not bear with that pain.

With his mother's permission, I approached him in order to help him. In his face you could see reflected the suffering and anguish. She told me that a very heavy object had fallen on his hand it almost crushed it. The doctor on duty had only given him painkillers. After three days the child was still in pain and the mother was desperate.

Then, I took at his hand and put it between mine, for a few minutes I closed my eyes and asked God to allow me to relieve him. When his hand went free from mine, and only in seconds, the little boy no longer felt the pain. His smile was back. The woman, surprised, thanked me with euphoria.

On another occasion, I was able to heal the wound of a peasant who worked on my uncles' farm. The man had, accidentally, injured his knee, working with a sharp knife. The blood was pouring out. I went home, brought thread and a needle to sew clothes, and proceeded to do the suture. When I put my hands on the lacerated knee, the pain disappeared.

The man asked me if I had used any kind of medication, because he didn't feel anything, even when the needle pierced his skin.

I could tell you many stories about the power I had with my hands, Vera; but the one that marked my life the most, was when my son became seriously ill. I knew I just needed to touch him and put my hands on his chest to heal him. He was just a baby and he was suffering from a painful lung disease.

The doctors said he would probably die. Days before, I had touched his chest many times without getting any result. I was desperate. I didn't understand why my hands didn't work. Then, I got so angry with the universe, with the almighty God, while questioning him what was the reason why I was not allowed to heal my own son.

After several attempts I realized I would not succeed, I was filled with rage and swore that I would never go back to that gift to heal other people. My son would die and I couldn't do anything.

The day the doctors said they couldn't do anything more for him, I stayed with him all night; according to them, he would not awake alive. I slept disconsolate. At dawn, I was surprised he was healthy and smiling. I could not explain what had happened. Could it be a miracle? or God had finally heard me. I will never know.

After what happened, everybody went crazy in the hospital. The doctors arrived; they didn't explain themselves how my baby was still alive; they said they could only attribute it to a miracle.

——Charif, how amazing! I would never have imagined it. You are a special being and I appreciate your friendship and your trust.

We had been almost four hours immersed in this conversation. He assured me that he had much more to tell me, but they were about to close the restaurant and we had to leave. I loved his story; it was touching and fantastic. I was perplexed, I would never have thought that I could meet such a kind of person.

——You, see ——, he said—— I want to ask you if we can go out for a drink tomorrow.

——Charif, I was waiting for you to ask me, ——I said excitedly. And, of course, I accepted immediately.

That night had been one of the most exciting evenings of my life. I was thirsty to know more about him. We said goodbye. I left for my house thinking that I've had the privilege of listening to his confidences. I prayed to God to keep his friendship; Charif was a unique person.

*****

The newspaper office was bursting of activity;

journalists came and went; the director was giving shouting orders, all related to the visit of a very famous actor. It was necessary to interview him and take pictures of him in the most important places in *Antigua*.

Xiomara and I were designated to cover the event. We arrived at the *Santo Domingo* hotel and that famous character was waiting for us at the restaurant-. We saw him and we, instantly, were amazed by its physique; it was an *Adonis*. We sat down to have some coffee. At the end of the interview, we took him for a walk in the city. He was delighted and excited; he wanted to take pictures from everywhere. He felt an admiration for *Antigua*.

He promised us next time he would film here. He was nice, but like all celebrities, elusive, sullen and with an immense ego. When we left the hotel, he said goodbye to us, forever. We did not see him again. We had good pictures. Xiomara and I appeared in some. Without a doubt, the testimony of a celebrity about *Antigua* would be a good report that we could exploit abroad. Mr. Castaneda congratulated us; he was very satisfied with our work.

Upon arriving at my cubicle, I realized that we had a very tight schedule, the next events and festivities were approaching.

Although, the work was exciting and gave me the opportunity to meet many interesting and famous people, I could not deny that some days more than others, it was very strenuous. That afternoon I left the office walking like a zombie due to fatigue.

*****

Charif called me to remind me of our appointment and even though I was exhausted, I went to my commitment. I was dying to hear the part of his story that he still hadn't told me.

My mother was in the kitchen giving some instructions to Dalila and my father was in his study room avidly reading a historical novel. The doorbell rang, it was sure it was Charif. I went forward to open it and invited him in. My mother went out to meet him; I introduced him to her and realized that she had liked him. He called my father, who came immediately to meet my new and original friend.

I showed him the house. He was thrilled to see those baskets of flowers that hung in each column of the corridor. He was fascinated by the traditional patio in the middle, and the fountain surrounded by tropical flowers and singing birds.

My mother exchanged some words with him, not so many because we had to leave soon. My father told him, he had been to Bogotá once, he had liked the city and the people. They were very polite and formal persons. At the end of the brief conversation we went to *Maya bar*, the place where we had met for the first time, that night, where I almost made a ridiculous scene.

Like every night, the place was full. There wasn't one single table available, until, we saw one at the end of the hall, which seemed to have been specially arranged for us, as it was a little out of the hustle and bustle, it would provide privacy.

When we sat down the waiter came to offer us the drink. The menus were already on the tablecloth. That time I wasn't going to drink *tequila*, I didn't want to talk about my sorrows anymore, I just wanted to hear the other part of Charif's story. So, we ordered a Merlot wine of Chilean origin.

Charif began by telling me that I had to know everything about his family since for him it was very important.

—This time I will tell you about my parents.

—They, Vera, met in Honda, a region of Tolima. It was during a trip to that town that Dad and Mom's younger brother, uncle Miguel, who, without imagining what was going to happen, invited his sister to the picnic. Dad and uncle Miguel were coworkers at the Iberian Stationery Company a famous business based in Bogotá; it was there that a friendship was born which would last a lifetime.

In Honda they stayed at the house of one of *Dad's* aunts, named Teresa. Mom was beautiful with her shiny wavy brown hair and her big dark eyes. As soon as *Dad* saw her, he fell in love with her, it was love at first sight. After that picnic, they were certain they would see each other again, due to the relationship between my father and uncle Miguel, who was, in this case, the cupid for the romance.

*****

The Iberian Stationery Company became their meeting point. In addition, it was the time in which they saw each other more. She lived near those stores and often went to chat with her brother; *Dad* was there almost always. That's how they became best friends and then became boyfriends.

They used to meet each other outside their house because my grandfather looked after his daughters in an exaggerated way, he did not allow anyone to visit them, let alone if they were his suitors. With a funny Arabic accent, he said: "he would shoot the *son of a bitch* who would approach them," the words sounded funny since in the Arab language the pronunciation is other, very different. *Dad* had no other way but to arrive accompanied by an entourage composed by *Mom's* brothers. According to my mother, when grandfather saw him, he turned around, but not before telling him he was returning. And with some anger, he headed for his room shouting that he was going to look for his weapon. Dad paled, but remained motionless; I think he was going to risk everything for the love of the woman he adored. That threat would never become real.

When my grandfather met him and knew he was a good man, he accepted him; after a few months, they were already planning the wedding. They married a radiant day in Bogotá. They had the permission of all the family, specially of my maternal grandparents. The wedding was Catholic, since his family had always been a Maronite Christian, in Lebanon.

Mom once told me that when I was born, my grandfather did not allow anyone to approach me. He wanted to do everything for me, give me the bottle and give me a mother's care; I was his spoiled and his most precious child. That's why I say I adore them? ——He concluded.

When Charif finished his story, I looked at him with admiration. Then, we engage in ourselves and leave aside the theme of his family.

——I love seeing you, ——he said——, looking me into my eyes.

That time I noticed him differently. He looked at me with desire; It showed me another phase of his personality. At that moment, I remembered the first date I had with Vincenzo and I was a little scared to fall back into a spider web, but I immediately knew Charif was far diverse from Vincenzo, and I should trust him. Then I felt ashamed with myself for having conceived that thought.

I liked that man very much. And, like any girl in a similar situation, I got out the best of my seductive personality: I spoke with my mouth, with my eyes, with my body. My body language was quite clear, it didn't need words.

He had a flirtatious smile. His bright eyes looked at me without blinking, as if he didn't want to miss a single detail of me. Without waiting for him, he got up from the table and stamped on my mouth, his first kiss. A pleasant shiver ran through my body. I felt in my stomach the famous butterflies that everyone talks about. I liked it and wanted to continue experiencing such a delicious sensation, so I started provoking him, to kiss me again.

The waiter arrived at that precise moment and proceeded to uncork the wine, meanwhile we both looked at each other with a repressed desire. Then we collided our glasses to toast for love; also, for the luck of having met and for the future.

They served us dinner and we only played with it, pretending to eat, we were more focused on our conversation and coquetry, than on anything else. If we were hungry it was of love and not from food, even though everything looked appetizing. Those in front of our table watched us and murmured something in between mischievous giggles. Love floated in the air.

After Charif paid the bill, we left in a hurry, like two lovers, who eagerly, wanted to make love. My fate was him. I would throw myself into the abyss without thinking about it, I was sure I wouldn't crash. He inspired me with the trust I never felt in Vincenzo.

The night and a beautiful moon, which shone like

never before, became accomplices and witnesses of our love. We walk hand in hand on those cobbled and somewhat lonely streets. We sat in a park to contemplate the infinite sky full of stars.

Charif took me by the hand and declared his love to me, first with a long, wet kiss, and then with a hug so strong, that he pulled me out to the last breath. Since that day, we never parted. I would live with my *last Lebanese* a true love, without deception or false promises.

I had been in Guatemala for more than a year and I was less regretful every day. The past no longer existed for me, and I was glad to be in my land, with my parents, my friend Rosa and, above all, with Charif, my true love.

In my work everything was going well. I couldn't be happier. Mr. Castaneda was satisfied with my work. I was scared of the idea that everything went so well and nothing bad happened. I was afraid of so much happiness, it seemed unreal to me.

*****

One day, my friend Rosa called me to tell me that when she was visiting the academy, she had met a man, as that funny clairvoyant of the turban had predicted her. He approached her and, without preamble, introduced himself and invited her for coffee. she was excited. The young man was from Utah and seemed it had been *loved at first sight*, just as the gypsy had said.

On another day, Rosa took her friend Warren to my house. We decided to go out to dinner with them. Through the conversation Charif and I liked him very much. He was a tall, blond man with blue eyes. His sense of humor was very similar to Charif's.

After six months of courtship he was already proposing marriage to her, it had been a lightning love, of those that only happened in soap operas. He was a good man, owner of large tracts of land in Utah.

*****

The night before the wedding I felt something strange in the environment, Charif also perceived it. There was a sepulchral silence, all over, the crickets did not squeak, it seemed that time had stopped; and, the moon, between black clouds, hid its brightness. We both had a bad feeling.

Suddenly, silence broke in with the howls of the dogs, as if something made them nervous. Charif, who was so sensitive to everything, hugged me. His expression betrayed him; I knew he sensed something was about to happen, something very wrong. However, immersed in the happiness of our love, we concentrate on filling ourselves with good vibes and ignoring our fears.

*****

The marriage took place in the Saint Joseph Cathedral of *Antigua*. The religious ceremony was brief. I was Rosa's godmother, and Charif, the groom's godfather. The party was held at the *Camino Real* hotel. When we arrived, there was a *Marimba* at the entrance; a percussion instrument, typical of Guatemala, similar to the xylophone, that played traditional melodies to cheered the entry of new married couple and of the guests.

Rosa looked gorgeous in her wedding dress; He wore a crown of white flowers on his head. Warren looked happy and very much in love. The tables were beautifully decorated. We set out to toast for the married couple so as to later enjoy the wide *repertoire* offered by a famous musical band: a bit of all genres and lots of tropical music.

Charif and I followed the dance after the couple opened it, and while we were dancing in the middle of the saloon, he whispered me he had a surprise for me. I had a hard time believing it could be the engagement ring, however, I didn't rule out that possibility; deep down I was almost certain he would ask me to marry him. The song ended and we headed to the table.

The atmosphere was favorable; and with great solemnity, he stood up to announce our commitment to all at the table. When I heard the good news, I almost fainted. He put a beautiful jade ring with diamonds on my finger. I couldn't speak out of emotion. My parents stayed silent, even though, I saw Mom was very excited, almost about to cry, and me also.

I understood the next bride would be me. I could not contain my joy. I knew I would be very happy. I just kissed him, because I had run out of words. All at the table raise their champagne glasses to toast for our wedding. But a second later the misfortune knocked on the door without being invited. A tragedy of apocalyptic dimensions broke out, and it would change forever the course of my life.

A strange noise invaded the place, it sounded like the footsteps of a giant that was approaching and, in doing so, made the earth thunder and trembled. Little by little the noise grew louder and louder. Some guests were scared and quickly left the place. Others stayed; they were curious to know what was happening. We sat without moving from the table, waited with fear, and trying to calm down.

Minutes later the earth began to shake and the roar grew even louder. It felt a strong, oscillating movement, it seemed that the ground danced roughly. Each time it moved more and more, until no one could be standing on their feet. An earthquake of catastrophic magnitude had broken out.

Shouts were heard inside the room and people stampeded with an expression of terror on their faces. Then, after a pause and a deadly silence, in a fraction of seconds, we heard that awful noise accompanied by a thunder, it seemed that the sky was about to fall on the city. The earth shook strongly, and everything creaked around us. The glasses, cups, and other things that were on the tables flew everywhere and fell to the ground shattering.

Charif tried to calm me down. I couldn't even stand up; the sway of the movement made me stagger, he held me so I did not fall to the ground. He told me to keep calm, it was an earthquake.

When we saw around us, my parents were gone, even though we had asked them not to move; They ignored it, and rushed out. It was already late; in the distance, I saw them running, and pushing everyone they found in their path. Panic had taken hold of them. A good number of people huddled at the door of the room blocking the passage to the other side. A human cork formed that did not let the desperate leave.

Everything became chaos. The screams announced the misfortune that was happening. Petrified, I saw how the movement of the ceiling caused a large lamp, in the middle of the room, wobble violently, until it fell on the people who were trying to protect themselves; some died immediately, they were smashed among heavy irons. Several wounded grabbed cloth napkins and dried the blood of their bodies; those who lay on the ground could not get up and would beg begged for help. Rosa and Warren had disappeared, just like my parents.

A second later, Charif alerted me with a shout and, pulling me away with an abrupt wrench, prevented me from another lamp it was about to fall on my head. Some people searched with fear acquaintances or relatives by their howls, and in the midst of chaos, we began to hear the sound of sirens in the distance.

With megaphones, the hotel managers, gave precise instructions so people would not stack at the exits, to avoid more accidents. Antigua was collapsing. Nature and the *Mayan* gods were punishing the inhabitants of a privileged city.

When we were able to go out into the street, we saw the enraged *Huangpu* volcano throwing rays and flames, the lava began to descend from the dome, like burning waves; we didn't know how far it would go. Distress was present; we ran to the sidewalk and started looking for my parents. We asked passersby, with a quick description, if they had seen them. But the shock didn't allow them to not even answer.

Many ran terrified trying to protect themselves from everything that threatened them. Also, we observed people standing in the middle of the street, praying and asking loudly for the salvation of their souls. Some indigenous people prayed in their dialect and asked their gods for protection.

There were ambulances everywhere carrying injured people to the hospital. It was all puzzling. When we didn't see my parents anywhere, we decided to return to the hotel. Along the way, we saw how some people had been trapped under the heavy stones of a wall that had collapsed. Fear invaded me. I was terrified to think that my parents could be there. We ran to see who was under the rubble.

As we approached, I could distinguish the color of mom's dress, but I had not yet seen her face. Near her, was a man who also seemed to wear a suit similar to my father's. I kept the failed hope they weren't my parents. It couldn't be.

I asked Charif, with a scream, if it was them. He begged me to calm down, to put myself in a safe place, first. But seeing his expression, I knew he was trying to prepare me for the worst.

In a second, it trembled stronger than the first time, and we both fell to the ground, a painting that was on an adjoining wall flew and injured my head.

Stunned and trying to stop the bleeding with my hand, I stood in front of the bodies of my parents, at that moment, the panic and pain took hold of us. There were no doubts, they were them. They lay inert. Their bodies were mistreated as if someone had seized them with stones, their heads were broken. They did not have the slightest expression of life.

I started crying uncontrollably. With screams of terror and anguish I called one of the nurses who were rescuing people. The man examined them, took their pulses and immediately told us they had died.

I started to cry in pain. Charif tried to prevent me from getting closer to their bodies. But it was impossible. I released myself abruptly and pounced on their lifeless bodies, trying to hug them and kiss their battered faces. Charif, unable to contain himself, exploded unhinged with grief, and in despair, he pulled me away. My parents' blood wetted all over my dress.

Their bruised bodies were taken by an ambulance to where hundreds of bodies of the victims of that misfortune were found. Ironically, I had to go immediately to the newspaper to cover the fatal news to inform the world.

*****

On my way to work, I spotted Rosa, and Warren; they were alive. We hugged each other for a long time and between bitter tears and tremors, I told them what had happened to my parents. Rosa, who was already desperate, got worse. I continued the path to my work escorted at all times by Charif and my friends.

Rosa came with me to Mr. Castaneda's office. We were glad to see that he was fine. I told him, in pain, that before I started my work I had to go home because my parents had died during the tragedy. With an expression of deep sadness, he told me he agreed, and amid my crying, he gave me his condolences. At that moment I felt supported by him and my coworkers.

My house was still standing. Upon entering we saw Dalila in the courtyard, she had dirt on his face. She told us, to not be alarmed, that everything was fine, the house, miraculously, had not suffered much damage. She said that when the earthquake started everything rocked as if it were a hammock; at that time, she was watering the flower baskets and the movements caused one of them to fall on her head; despite that, she only had a slight wound.

I would have to tell Dalila that my parents had

died. After so many years working for them, I know she would suffer with that news. The first reaction she had was to lowered her head, and with a great sorrow, lock himself in her bedroom.

After a few hours she came out of her bedroom with her face transformed and her eyes swollen from so much crying. She stated, she wanted to collaborate with the funeral preparations.

My parents were buried in the family pantheon. The mass celebration was officiated by Father Sánchez at the Cathedral, which didn't suffer that much.

The earth was still moving every now and then; There were still small aftershocks. Nature, for no reason, took revenge on everyone. The earthquake had left desolation, houses and buildings collapsed, in ruins. And what cannot be repair or replaced: the loss of loved ones and the deep pain that it causes. A few days later, the whole world sent humanitarian aid for the victims.

I felt alone. The people I loved so much were no longer by my side, I was only comforted to have Charif close to me. Our love commitment was still alive.

He moved to my house. We talked about getting married as soon as possible. His proposal had only one condition: the wedding should be in Bogotá, Colombia.

Antigua was, nothing more, than a mountain of rubble; and, all of its inhabitants committed to work on its reconstruction.

After three months we started the wedding plans. I was saddened that my parents were not with us. My duel was not over yet; I didn't even know how long it would last me; probably a lifetime. The truth was that the wound was open; maybe the wedding would help partially to relieve my grief.

Every time a catastrophe of that magnitude passed, I questioned God. I wanted him to explain to me why things like that happened and why he didn't protect his children like a good father would do in the face of danger.

My faith staggered and it had become an obsession to know where my parents were, if they were well, if in the hereafter pain didn't exist as here on earth, if there were angels, if there was a heaven, and a hell. To know that, only a shaman could help me; in my country, there were many who were not charlatans, however, my desire was against my religious beliefs. Father Sanchez said it was a sin; but in spite of everything my religion commanded, I could not marry or leave Guatemala without being sure that my father and mother were at peace.

*****

I called Rosa. She told me she knew a *Shaman* in Petén, an indigenous descendant of the great *Mayas* who lived in the middle of the jungle; with vast knowledge inherited from the wisdom of their ancestors. He was an intermediary between gods and men. He could guess, heal, and enter the world of the dead. His name was Vicente and his nick name: *Don Chente.*

When I decided to go, I thought to request permission from the church; but since I knew that Father Sánchez would not give it to me, I went to the Cathedral, and on my knees, I asked God for forgiveness. When I left, I reunited with Rosa and Charif, we needed to plan the trip to Petén, which incidentally, would be a great adventure, especially for him.

Rosa had been there before. In Guatemala it was not uncommon for people to consult a *Shaman*. They were not seen as satanic or evil people, but as healers of the soul, benevolent beings possessing a gift that allowed us to find the perfect harmony between body, spirit and mother earth.

We went to the travel agency and bought the tickets. It would be a short trip that we would do in a small airplane. We would land in Flores, a municipality in where the park is located, which is one of the most important archaeological discoveries and urban centers of the pre-Columbian Mayan civilization; located precisely in the department of Petén.

For Charif it was quite an experience to see those imposing Mayan temples in the middle of the jungle. First of all, the temple of the Great Jaguar, a pyramid 47 m high, which was known as the gateway to the underworld. I was excited that Charif would accompany me to find out about the status of my parents in the hereafter. It was a rainy season, so between thunder and lightning we set out for Tikal.

We arrived at Flores, departmental capital of Petén, also known as Isla de Flores and anchored in Lake Petén Itzá.

We landed in well; but when we got off the plane, we felt that the humidity suffocated us. A torrential rain was falling and we were getting soaking wet. We took a taxi that took us to the hotel recommended by the travel agency. It was rustic. We were assigned a cabin that had three beds. The next day we would go early to look for *Don Chente*.

It wouldn't be a romantic night for Charif and me, because we would have to share the room with Rosa, but it was a fun day that brought us back to the time of the school rides.

The cabin was spacious. There were three beds in a row and a small closet. The floor was of brick and thatched roof. We had inspected the place thoroughly for bugs; Despite that, Rosa alerted us with a loud shout: a huge tarantula was moving stealthily through the bathroom tiles. Rosa had turned pale. And when we were thinking about how to help her eliminate the unsuspecting arachnid, a huge shoe crushed him in one blow. We laughed at Rosa's reaction, hoping that another similar bug wouldn't visit us during the night.

We left our backpacks in a rustic wooden furniture and went to dinner, we were tired and hungry. The restaurant tables were simple, they had brightly colored embroidered tablecloths. Everything around us was as colorful as the jungle itself. The menu was purely typical food, national beer and natural fruit beverages. Charif was enchanted in eating *tamales*. The dessert were *jocotes* in honey, a true delight.

When it came time to sleep, we had a hard time doing so. Noises did not let us fall asleep. Roars could be heard everywhere, and the sounds were similar to laughter out of tune. Then, somebody told us it was the monkeys. We also heard footsteps of animals that appeared to be felines, perhaps those of a wildcat or a jaguar. But with all that, fatigue overcame us and we ended up sleeping lulled by the sounds of the jungle.

The next morning everything was wet, a great storm had hit the whole place and there were puddles where we passed.

After breakfast, and a hot cup of *chocolate*, we went to look for the guide, Jaime Hernández would be the one who would accompany us on our journey.

As planned by the guide, that day we would walk through the jungle; and would arrive almost at sunset to our destination. *Don Chente* lived in a small village in the middle of nowhere. He was well known, and surely, Jaime would take us to him without a problem.

On the way we saw a huge amount of tropical flora, looked like the earthly paradise described in the bible. The path was full of huge *ceibas,* centenary trees, which in its trunks, entangled gigantic vines with immense leaves that made the light enter dimly.

The guide man, with his *machete,* was cutting the lianas to open the way. It felt a wet freshness which was not annoying. In the distance there was a stream which according to Jaime, was not deep, and therefore, we could cross it.

While we were walking and chatting, monkeys of different species offered us a show, fooling around, they were hanging from the tree branches. Suspended, they swayed from side to side. Some jumped from branch to branch and ate fruits of all kinds, they were funny gymnasts. We could also see the national bird of Guatemala, the emblematic *Quetzal,* proudly wearing its phosphorescent green feathers, and its long and delicate tail. Jaime told us it was the sacred bird of the *Maya.*

Shortly after, we jumped out of scare that caused us a snake of bright colors that appeared from nowhere, it looked like he was in a hurry because he ran rapidly to hid under a big stone. Jaime assured that he was not poisonous and that we should not fear him.

——"Surely, she fears us more,"——he added calmly.

It was already getting dark when we ran into another stream; It was a little wider than the previous one. After crossing it, we would rest for a while; We were close to getting to where *don Chente* lived.

We sat on some flat stones on the shore to take a little rest. We drank some water from our canteens. Rosa took some loaves of chicken out of her jacket that would give us more energy. We were immersed in a quiet talk, when we heard the hoarse and cavernous roar of an animal. Jaime, putting his index finger to his mouth, told us to be silent, and to remain calm, and still.

It was a huge jaguar, that within a few meters, watched us with a fixed and curious look, while he was drinking water from the stream. The three of us were fascinated, and at the same time thrilled to see such a beautiful creation. But the fear was present too.

It was astonishing. Within minutes, the immense feline walked with parsimony in the opposite direction to ours. When we were sure he had gone away completely, we exhaled a deep sigh. Jaime explained that he was probably satisfied, otherwise, we would have become his prey, a big dinner, he said laughing.

—This is the jungle. Anything can happen ——he stressed.

After that experience, I did not know if to entered the habitat of jaguars, monkeys, pumas, vipers, birds of all species and many other animals, had been a good idea. Charif didn't seem very convinced, even so, he didn't complain. We walked half an hour more and we reached a clearing in which we could see around ten huts.

——"Good evening"——Jaime said.

He then, communicated with those who were there in an unintelligible dialect for us. After this, he left, walking slowly, and a small man who had long white hair, and a face full of wrinkles, boarded him. He was *don*

Chente, who, kindly, came out to welcome us in a Spanish with an air of indigenous accent.

He led us to his hut and asked us all kinds of questions. While he was talking, he smoked a pipe with tobacco that smelled rotten. He urged us to start, as soon as possible, since the next day he would have to get up early to go to the city.

Inside his hut there was a bed and two hammocks, an improvised handmade kitchen with firewood and two white plastic chairs.

After a moment, he invited us to smoke his tobacco; He said it was part of the ceremony. He also asked us to take a couple of sips of a thin broth that he had poured into small containers. The transparent soup was served to all of us.

I didn't want to taste it, but I had to; there was no other alternative. Charif and Rosa took the first sip; I immediately noticed their gestures of repulsion. The *calducho (thin broth),* was more bitter than the gall itself. *Don Chente* said it would help us to enter the world of the dead and open our levels of consciousness to finally see the spirits of my parents.

A few minutes after, I felt a spasm in my stomach. I had to go to the bathroom to vomit. Charif and Rosa had their faces contorted and were frowning them as if they were chewing a lemon.

Subsequently, the man asked us to go to sit around a bonfire that burned with splendor.

Drums and species of *maracas* accompanied a song that *Don Chente* sang to call his spiritual guides. Suddenly, I began to feel that everything around me was moving slowly.

The colors of the jungle started to glow in phosphorescent tones, they move in a strange way, as if they had electricity. The brightness was so intense that it blinded my eyes, I had to close them for a moment.

Don Chente, in his native dialect, and at the rhythm of a drum, called the spirits of my parents by their names. I never knew how he had heard their names; it was a mystery that I preferred not to solve.

I could not measure the time that passed, nor the dimension or earthly distance. I only remember that I saw Charif and Rosa with a halo of very bright light on their heads; I also saw rays coming out of their bodies. Everything was strange and surrealistic.

In a semi-conscious state, I could see my parents near the hut of *Don Chente*. They walked towards us smiling and holding hands as if death had failed to separate them. They looked like of flesh and blood. Rays of white light emanated from their bodies, as if they were angels. Then, we saw a jaguar who accompanied them; It seemed it was not dangerous, it appeared to be like their pet.

They approached and communicated through our minds. Their mouths did not articulate words, but their voices were heard as echoes that came mixed with the breeze. We all became mute of surprise when in a soft and with a delicate voice, they said in unison:

——*My daughter.*

Their voices filled me with peace and love. His figures became fragile, it seemed that the wind made them dance in an ethereal movement.

They told me they were in a beautiful place, where there was no pain, no old age. Everyone there was young. They looked happy. They asked me not to worry.

They assured me they would always be present in

my life, although I could not see them. They advised me to take good care of myself. My father's spirit added:

—*We are in a place very similar to paradise. There is no evil here. Heaven is not as they paint it on earth, much less hell; after death there are only beings of light and goodness. There are no punishments for anyone. We are all at peace and there is an unceasing happiness.*

I listened in amazement, when my mother's spirit intervened:

——*We still haven't seen the great father of the universe. They say it is everywhere: in the beautiful flowers of the immense garden, in the trees, in the tweet of the birds, in all the animals that walk with us without harming us. Here, daughter, there are no diseases, no doubts or tribulation. We lead a perfect life in complete brotherhood. You can be calm. We love you.*

Suddenly, they shut up. His figures gradually faded away in a masterful flight, as if the wind were leading them to infinity. My gaze followed them as far as possible. After that incredible moment, I felt a peace I had never experienced before.

Don Chente explained that through vomit, I had expelled everything bad, what tormented me, what my body didn't need. He ended by telling me he had fulfilled his mission. That made me feel relieved. Healed in my being, there was no longer sadness, it was a spiritual therapy. I was grateful to Charif and Rosa, also to Jaime and, above all, to *Don Chente*, they had all made that happen. I would never forget it.

The jaguar had also left with my parents' spirits. *Don Chente* told us that he was a *Nagual*, a spirit with which people are born to help them, protect them and guide them throughout their lives. The *Nagual* also helped *Don Chente* to communicate better with the spiritual world, and many times, he could take the form of his own *Nagual*, be it a jaguar or an eagle. It was an ancestral wisdom, which we could hardly understand.

After several hours and without feeling sick, we went to sleep in a hut that had two cots and two hammocks. We fell like ripe pears from a tree. We experienced great peace and also immense exhaustion.

The next morning, we felt the heat of the sun's rays, which entered through all the cracks in the walls of the hut. We were looking for *Don Chente* to thank him, but we no longer found him. The villagers said that he had become his *Nagual* and was wandering around. In other words, in the jaguar we had seen near the stream, maybe.

With all those wonderful treasured experiences, and with peace to know that my parents were well, wherever they were, we set out back to rest and prepare to make the trip to Guatemala City the next day, from which we would head towards Antigua.

It was curious how my sadness had dissipated forever. Charif and I felt healthy and ready to embark on the great journey to our future city: Bogotá.

***

Charif called his mother to give him the good news. In a few days we would leave for Bogotá. She, and my sisters-in-law had been communicating often to see if we were well.

My mother-in-law had expressed her desire to celebrate the wedding at the Lebanese Club in Bogotá, the Lebanese style. It would be a great event. I had never attended a Lebanese wedding, so I had no idea how it was celebrated, it seemed that it was not so different from a traditional Catholic wedding. I was very curious to know how it was going to be. In the long run, I would not have cared if it had been celebrated under a tree, the only relevant thing was that I was sure of my love for Charif and what he felt for me.

Doña Raquel, my mother-in-law, told us that the whole family was waiting for us with open arms; she also told us that living in Colombia would allow us to breathe a different air and move away from so many painful memories; maybe, she was right, but the encounter with my parents had been so healing that there was no more pain; I knew they were happy.

The truth is that I no longer had anything to do in Guatemala, besides my friend Rosa and Warren, and a few other people I knew, I felt that no other link joined me to that land. My life in Guatemala was buried in the fatal past. Without my parents, my only family was Charif and his family. I thought that moving to Bogotá would open a new world to us and help erase that dark day from our minds.

***

He had always been anxious to write a book about Charif's Lebanese grandparents. Every time he told me some of his family anecdotes, I felt inspired to capture it on paper. Writing was going to be easier in Colombia, because there I could access to the testimonies of some of his relatives, such as his mother or maternal uncles who were still alive.

It would be very interesting to know how Antonio and María Abosaid, Charif's maternal grandparents, had arrived from Lebanon to Bogotá. I considered the best title for my work would be *The Last Lebanese,* referring to Charif, the main protagonist of my story. After a few minutes of maturing the idea, I jumped for joy like a little girl thinking that I could turn my dream into reality.

I talked to Rosa about my plans. I also informed Mr. Castaneda, who was not very happy for me to leave for Colombia, but it was my destiny. Rosa couldn't help it, the melancholy invading her; that is why, from that day on, we tried to spend as much time as possible together and, thus, take advantage of the little we had left.

I notified Dalila of the changes that were coming and I informed her that, unfortunately, she would have to go home, I gave her a good retire pension, for all the years she worked with such dedication, for us. She was very sad about the news, and at the same time, happy for me.

As for my parents' house, I planned to sell it, but Rosa and Warren wanted to rent it; that made me very happy, I would not be separated from what had been my home and that of my parents.

The day of departure arrived. Tears ran like rivers. It hurt me to say goodbye to the people I truly appreciated at work and others very close, such as Father Sánchez, Warren, and, of course, my friend Rosa.

The reconstruction of Antigua was going well. Every day that passed you could tell this beautiful city was being reborn among the rubble.

I was leaving a magical place of Shamans, of tales and ancient legends. While saying goodbye to that majestic and treacherous volcano, I felt I was leaving my land with much affliction.

Charif called the travel agency and bought without hesitation two tickets to Bogotá. One way. We would travel the next day.

We left at noon from Guatemala. It would take us a few hours to reach our final destination. I thought sadly, this time, I would leave my land forever.

THIRD PART

Reynaldo Armas (Time Traveler)

We were already close to Bogotá and the trip had been pleasant. A few minutes before landing, I observed a city surrounded by the majestic greenery that makes up the Bogotá savanna and the imposing mountains that are part of the eastern *cordillera* (mountain chain).

Upon leaving the airport there was a group of people who greeted us with enthusiastic gestures. It was the Fernández Abosaid family: Mom, sisters, nephews, brothers-in-law, and there was a toddler too.

When we approached, everyone ran to hug us, it seemed that this warm welcome would never end. You could tell it was a very close family, full of love and joy.

My mother-in-law had wet eyes out of emotion and wrapped me in kisses, when I saw her, I could see how beautiful she was; She had gray hair, and few wrinkles on her face, large brown-brown almond shaped eyes, an aquiline nose and thick lips without being bulging. Her face was harmonious.

My sisters-in-law were three in total. Claudia had black hair, white skin, small eyes and a slim body. According to Charif, she was the one who looked most like his father. Luisa, on the other hand, was a woman with abundant and wavy hair, brown color and light green eyes, of medium height. Her features were very Lebanese. The smallest of all wore very short hair, although she was a very quiet woman, she had a spontaneous and sweet smile that always illuminated her face, her name was Jackie.

In total there were four children, Charif was the eldest. We left the airport in an uproar. Everyone talked at the same time trying to decide what to do, when they arrived. We were heading towards the house where Charif had grown up.

The house was medium-sized. On the first floor, it had a dining room with a small fireplace in the middle, then the living room, and a bathroom, in the hall. A half-wall separated the breakfast room with the kitchen. In the back there was a small garden with white giant roses, and a miniature avocado tree. On the second floor there were four spacious bedrooms, three bathrooms, and a study.

When my mother-in-law was widowed, her daughter Claudia and her husband Daniel moved to live with her to keep her company and help her with household tasks. Daniel was a doctor of Colombian origin. He was a good man, a little quiet. In that house the children of the marriage were born.

My mother-in-law's brothers, men and women, also lived very close. Everything had been planned so that the family was always united, as was usual in that culture.

The neighborhood, which was once residential, had now become a commercial area. That was an advantage for them because they had everything at hand. In the opposite corner there was a supermarket, close enough to get the necessary. It was a simple life, somewhat routinely, but very comfortable.

My family, I say mine, because it would soon be forever; had prepared a Lebanese meal to welcome us. *Dona* Raquel had learned from her mother all the secrets and recipes of Arabic food, which was very tasty and healthy; It had consistent flavor and was tempting to any palate.

The dining room table was adorned with delicious dishes, such as *kibbe, tabbouleh, hummus*, pita bread, and lamb. One that I will never forget is *baklava*, the recipe was from grandfather Antonio, a type of pillow-shaped cake, made from puff pastry, stuffed with pistachio and honey-covered nuts.

Charif brought me a plate, and as a child in a candy store, I didn't know what to choose. I wanted to try everything.

In the background an Arab music sounded that harmonized perfectly with the food. From one moment to another the rhythm changed and gave way to the Colombian chords; which meant that the family also felt proud of their South American roots.

The doorbell rang. They were the uncles who arrived just at the moment when the feast began. The women were very nice. Lucy, who always had an anecdote to tell, was short and tanned. He had huge amber eyes, under thick eyelashes. Aunt Luisa was less talkative. She was tall and thin. She had black hair and penetrating eyes of the same color. Some uncles were missing that I would soon meet. One of them was uncle Alberto.

The dinner was very pleasant. Everyone made me feel like family. I did not perceive cold or hostile attitudes. My mother-in-law went out of care for me, and after the entertainment, showed us the room we would occupy. That affection I felt, slightly offset the absence of my parents, who were in my mind day and night.

Some people of Bogotá usually drink spirits to mitigate low temperatures or to accompany family gatherings. *Aguardiente* is an aniseed drink, quite strong, made from cane; and since it was a typical cold Bogota night and we also had a lot much to celebrate, that liquor accompanied our celebration; However, Charif and I did not drink it, we preferred to retire to our room, we were exhausted and we just wanted to rest. So, once we arrived, we put our heads on the fluffy pillows and fell asleep. There was no space or desire to make love.

In the morning, a warm sun, without being abrasive, heated our bodies. The day began with a cup of the famous Colombian coffee, so appreciated in the world, and with a tour of the city.

The Colombian capital is cooler than Antigua; It is a climate that I have always loved because I feel it gives me energy. When I went out to the street, I saw the pretty trees that line the wide sidewalks and that green in their parks, which are all over the city; to the east, I admired the imposition of its hills. Bogotá was designed to the delight of those who visit it, and for its inhabitants.

The first stop we made was at the sanctuary of *Monserrate*; a place for pilgrimage, since colonial times. It is located on the eastern hills at 3152 m high. We ascended by funicular and from there we contemplated the entire city. Already at the top, we headed towards the *basilica* where the *Fallen Lord of Monserrate* is; there, I kept silent and with much fervor, I prayed for all the people I love: for my friends, family, and enemies too.

Then we went to the Gold Museum (*Museo del Oro*), a place that houses relics of pottery and gold from indigenous cultures of pre-Columbian times. Next to this, there is one of the many craft markets that abound in Bogotá; There, I did not know where to look, there were so many beautiful things to buy, especially, beautiful handbags made by the indigenous *Wayú* community, which had a design and colorfulness that could be the envy of any famous designer.

In the historic center of *La Candelaria* I moved to the 18th century when I saw the colonial-style houses with their balconies and wooden carved doors. It was also interesting to know the *Capitol*, which is the mayor's office, the *Palace of Justice* and *the House of Nariño*, the official residence of the president of the Republic, located in another of the emblematic sites of the Colombian capital: the *Plaza Bolívar*, a place where thousands of doves flutter happily, among themselves and tourists.

The day was short, it was not enough to discover the wonders that the city offers. I still had a lot to know, but I would have a lifetime to do it, or so I thought.

We arrived home late, after a delicious dinner in *Usaquén*; which is a neighborhood of colonial architecture and bohemian atmosphere that has a small square with a fountain in the middle, surrounded by exclusive restaurants. In that place, people enjoy walking through its picturesque streets.

And like any other woman, I couldn't resist; I went to three stores to buy things I didn't need, but in the end, I loved what I bought. Charif just laughed. We were so happy. The nightmares of the past were about to disappear forever, now I was remembering my parents with less pain. Even one day I thought I heard mom's voice telling me:

—Calm down, Vera. Everything will be fine, enjoy

your new life——. maybe I just imagined it, but I rejoiced in it.

Before sleeping, Charif insisted that next day we should go to find an apartment for both of us.

When we got up, the first thing we did was to check the newspaper, while this was happening, my sisters-in-law were talking about the dresses they would wear for the wedding; My mother-in-law silently watched them carefully, and smiled.

We could see in the newspaper a good number of apartments that interested us.

After visiting about four, we chose one that had two bedrooms. From the moment we entered we fell in love with the kitchen, which was wide, the windows over-looked the park and it had a lot of light. It was newly re-modeled. The floors were all wood and the building was very well maintained.

The real estate lady, seeing our enthusiasm, knew im-mediately that we would take it without persuading us, so we filled out the forms, and without hesitation, we gave her a down payment.

I, spontaneously, hung myself on Charif's neck to thank him and gave him, maybe, a thousand kisses. Everything seemed to be going perfectly. The apartment had what we needed and was located in a quiet area. In addition, the rent was not burdensome. Later, Charif said that it was time to organize the wedding, and for that, my mother-in-law would have to help me, who knew very well how to plan a Lebanese wedding.

When we got home, we shared the apartment's find, which for us was the ideal. She excitedly told us:

——It's time to organize the wedding——, and went to the kitchen singing a love tune.

***

During lunch, we had an extensive conversation about the wedding and all aspects that could not go unnoticed. When we concluded, my mother-in-law went to the studio announcing that she had a surprise for me. From a scribe he pulled out a beautiful little box with a pair of gold earrings with pink pearls, surrounded by diamonds, that originally belonged to grandma María, and would now pass to the third generation.

In Lebanese culture, before the wedding, it is a tradition for the mother of the groom to give her daughter-in-law a gift. When I received the gift, I was filled with emotion, I could not contain my joy and thanked her for having that nice detail with me; to accept it was to confirm my commitment to love his son, even after death. She smiled and winked at me. I ran to my room and put them on. They had that exotic design typical of the ancient Arab jewels. I was ecstatic.

With the present I received, the first step was already taken. I had something from my mother-in-law that meant a lot to her and now to me. What followed was to choose a wedding dress. Finally, the visit to the club to learn about its facilities and finalize details such as the menu and other details.

The next day, we both went to see some dresses at exclusive and tasteful places in Bogotá.

I tried on a half dozen dresses and I decided for a peach colored one. It was perfect; My mother-in-law liked it a lot. We were a little hungry and were also cold, so we thought it was good idea to eat an *Ajiaco,* a typical soup made with chicken pieces, different types of potatoes, *Guasca* leaves, capers, avocado, rice, and milk cream. My taste for Colombian food grew more and more each day, I specially love the *arepas* (tortillas).

In that coming and going, my heart was full of happiness. I already had the love of my life, a family that loved me too, a beautiful city that welcomed me, open hearted. What more could I ask for.

We return home with giant bags. My sisters-in-law were waiting anxiously to see everything we had acquired. That night I saw Charif full of enthusiasm and happier than ever. The day was approaching and I was nervous as a young girl. I had already turned thirty and it was not possible that this was happening to me. Charif was forty-five years old, and two divorces. Of those marriages were born three children who, of course, would attend our wedding. There were no secrets between us; Well, that was what I believed.

*****

One beautiful afternoon, a few days before the wedding, Charif and I were sitting on the lawn of a park near the house; when suddenly, a *Ferrari* car drove by with a middle-aged man as a driver, and when he saw Charif, stopped at once. The man surprised, got off the car to greet him with enthusiasm. After a long hug, he gave me a short look with curiosity. Charif smiling told him:

—Roberto, how are you doing? I introduce you to Vera, my *fiancée*. She is from Guatemala.

—I am delighted to meet you! —he said shaking my hand—. What a beautiful bride, Charif! —he added mischievously.

—How do you like our country, Vera?

—It fascinates me. Every day I discover something wonderful. It's a country full of surprises, history, beauty

——I said smiling.

——And, tell me, how is my dear friend Charif treating you?

——I cannot complain. He is an easy man to love, he is a great person. I hope this answers your question ——I smiled.

——Brother ——he said——, I didn't know you had already matured.

Charif answered nothing and changed the subject. He seemed nervous, as if this encounter with his old friend disturbed him.

I didn't know what secrets that man kept of my future husband; but I was sure that Charif, sooner or later, would have to tell me what part of his life he was hiding.

After a brief conversation with Roberto, Charif and I, said goodbye to him with a hug; I didn't think he was a bad person, however, there was something I didn't like of him.

You could tell Roberto had money at full hands. We saw him pass in front of us, inside that expensive brand-new car, saying goodbye as if we were never going to see him again, and so it was. After that casual encounter, he disappeared from Charif's life forever.

When we left the park; and on my way home, I asked Charif who this individual was. Hesitating a little, he promised he would tell me a story he had decided to reserve for himself, because he was afraid I would think badly of him; but, that at the same time, he believed that I should know it, because it was part of his past, and it was about some disorderly years he had lived during his youth.

***

Roberto was a relative of a friend of Charif; they had met in their wanderings by the trendy nightclubs of that time. It was the time when Colombia was dominated by drugs and drug trafficking.

Roberto was a lower ranking boss in the Colombian mafia, although he was not among the most important, he was recognized and respected in those circles. He and his brothers entered the narcotics business as part of the famous *Medellin cartel*.

When Charif told me about who his friend was, I wanted to run away; but he assured me that although Roberto was engaged in illicit business, he had never been involved in drug trafficking, and that it only had to do with him when they shared in meetings or parties.

Of course, he confessed that, driven by curiosity, he had tried cocaine but was never addicted to the drug. He assured me that, after he overcame those years of folly, he had not used any narcotics again. In addition, he decided to move away forever from the world of drugs because he had a very serious problem with a friend of Roberto.

A little angry, I claimed him for not telling me that part of his life. He begged me to continue trusting him, and insisted that the reason he hadn't told me was because he was ashamed. He always assured me that this episode of his life had been silly, stupid due to immaturity and that, fortunately, he had left on time.

I believed. He knew that Charif wouldn't be able to do something like that; he was a man of values, who could never have become a gangster, even if he had acquaintances of that kind. I suppose that in Colombia in those days it was difficult not to have a relative, a friend or a neighbor who was not involved in the business; In addition, I understood that he was young and that his immaturity had led him to the forbidden.

—I'm going to tell you a story so you know why I stopped going to Roberto and what was the reason why I decided to end that friendship abruptly —he said, while he took my hand.

Roberto and I met from time to time in order to go out. He seemed to be a good person, friendly and very generous, he paid my bills every time we went out. There were no boring moments with him. Besides, he was always surrounded by beautiful women.

One night we went to a disco, before leaving his apartment we had inhale some cocaine. When we arrived at the place, the security men greeted him with great respect and allowed us to pass immediately. The queuing people watched us curiously; some seemed envious; others, admired. The truth is that we were treated like royalty.

It was close to two in the morning. *Coca* did not allow us to be sleepy, just to feel energetic and euphoric; under its effects, we believed ourselves the owners of the world.

The site was full of beautiful girls who swarmed like bees near the flowers, that is, women attracted to money and drugs. Among them were TV presenters, models, actresses and others that appeared to be exit from expensive brothels.

The music sounded loud. A beautiful hostess accompanied us to the table they had reserved for Roberto and his friends. I felt comfortable, because, believe it or not, that man has great charisma and a gentle way of treating you —he clarified—. After a few minutes, the beautiful girl took us to the table, *Cristal* champagne and *Dom Peri-*

gnon, and Blue Label whiskey bottles were ready for us. The man was treated as if he were the king of the night. Everything seemed to be going well, too well. I couldn't imagine that my life would be in danger that night ——Charif said——. I remember, seated next to me, to a very pretty girl from Sweden. She had long legs, platinum mane, deep blue eyes and very white skin. It seemed she had liked me. She was flirting with me openly.

I got up to go to the bathroom. Two friends of Roberto who were at the table did the same. While washing my hands I perceived those men did not take my eyes off me; I felt intimidated, their looks were penetrating and cold. My blood froze.

One of them approached me. He reached into the pocket of his jacket and pulled out a gun, which he then put in my temple. The people who were there, without saying a word, left in a hurry. I managed to think that that it would be the last day of my life, the minutes became eternal and, while I felt the cold barrel of the gun in my head, the man warned me that I could not engage in any dialogue with the Sweden girl who had been flirting with me all night.

I promised him that I would not do it, and assured him that I would retire from the *discotheque* when I returned to my table. Without going into explanations, I said goodbye to Roberto. He was surprised, and in order not to arouse suspicion, I used a family affair as an excuse.

I never told him anything that had happened that night. I wanted to continue living. With Roberto as a friend and with his chaotic life, I was in danger; that's why I decided to leave his bond. At first it hurt me, because he is a generous man and has a big heart; besides,

I had fun with him. But that bad moment had made me reacted, and I left that life of excesses, in which, little by little, I was getting into. That experience almost takes my life. For that reason, Vera, there is nothing to worry about. I learned the lesson and all remained in the past, one I will not repeat.

After that story, I stayed calm, I knew that Charif was telling me the truth, and it had only been a mistake of youth. He had no bandit soul, quite the opposite. So, I thought that the most convenient thing was to turn the page and I never talked with him about that matter again.

***

The time has come to meet the children of Charif. They were lovely. There were no frictions between us. They had their own interests and did not want to get into our lives. They were teenagers and what mattered most at the time were their friends. The boys lived with their mothers and one of them already lived alone.

We went to the Lebanese Club. It was a nice place with ample facilities. It was the most suitable place to perform the wedding. It had an expert chef who knew about Lebanese cuisine. He had come from Lebanon many years ago and had stayed in Colombia to work at the club.

After talking with the manager, we went to see the lounges and chose the smallest one, the most welcoming. We didn't need anything too big; the wedding would be intimate so there would be few guests.

However, my mother-in-law was determined to make it as in the tale of the *Arabian nights*; she wanted Arabic music and dancers dressed in typical Lebanese costumes. A buffet strictly in line with its culture. This type of party was called *Zaffe*; it is characterized by a pompous reception for the bride and groom, a march in which they participate, in addition to them, dancers, men with lances, drums, trumpets and bagpipes, also belly dancers.

In that celebration, all the guests, and family pay a tribute to the bride and groom, and make the future wife feel like a queen surrounded by music and bustle.

We left everything ready. The wedding would be the first week of the following month, we just needed to send the invitations and decide the decoration of the place. It would be an unforgettable event.

While the long-awaited moment arrived, we took care of our apartment, furnishing, and decorating it with beautiful and original details. Charif felt sad because his Lebanese grandparents would not be at the wedding. He insisted that I should write a story to tell the adventures they had lived in their journey from Lebanon to Colombia, he wanted to take that book to the grave; he would also teach his children, through the example of his grandparents, a couple united in love, and the struggle to achieve their dream.

With a hug that lasted an eternity, I promised to help him   on   this. And, as to start building that dream, I thought the most convenient thing for our honeymoon was to visit Beirut.

That would be the ideal place, to know more about their culture, we would also take advantage of the trip to inquire on the lives of our grandparents. Charif didn't know much about it. Only that they were from a village called Baissour, located on Mount Lebanon, a mountainous region north of Beirut. And for I needed to know more about the old couple to start writing the book, one day I asked him about our honeymoon:

——Well, love, we have to go on a wedding trip anyway——. He, for a moment, remained silent and in answering, suggested:

——Vera, why don't we better choose a less troubled place? Travel agencies never recommend Lebanon as a safe travel destination.

——But then, how do you intend me to write a book, if I don't have access to the true sources? ——I said in anguish.

——My mother and my uncles can be a good source, ——he said—— trying to convince me.

——Yes. But it is not the same as going to the place where your grandparents were born, and talking to the people who knew them, although, probably, many must be older ——I finished arguing——. It's not the same, Charif, I beg you to think about it. We need to travel! Is it so hard to understand it? ——I objected.

——It's all right, Vera. I don't want this to be a reason for discussion ——he told me calmly. But first I will have to find out how things are there. I wouldn't like to die during our honeymoon ——he replied amusingly.

——I agree, Charif——.There is nothing else to talk about. After the wedding, if we can, we will travel to Lebanon. I'm dying to see Lebanon ——I said with great enthusiasm.

To which Charif just grimaced and shook his head in disapproval by adding:

——There is no doubt, you must be crazy, love!

But I continued with my folly, and to convince him, I promised him that the book would be dedicated to his mother, his grandparents and, especially, to him.

We didn't talk about it again, there were a few days left before the big celebration. I wanted so much to live that experience.

***

While the big day arrived, we traveled to the famous Colombian eastern plain (*el Llano*). We wanted to see this immense plain of infinite horizons, listen to their music and taste the famous meat to the *Llanero* style, the pride of that region.

It was five in the morning when we left for our destination. The farm we would stay was located in the heart of the plain; far from the urban center, it bordered with the *Meta* and *Vichada* departments, near an indigenous reserve which was in the middle of nowhere. The nearest village was about five hours away.

We took off in three cars and we carried the necessary provisions for six people, which would last ten days: the uncles of Charif, owners of the farm, their two children and us, were aboard. The trip would take us about twelve hours. The last town we would pass through was called *Puerto Gaitán*; from there we would travel through the savanna.

When I saw all that vastness, it remembered me of the African savanna, it was very similar; a green ocean, with an infinite horizon, that seemed endless.

There was no paved road. Charif, who had already been there many years ago, said that to avoid getting lost, they had to follow the landmarks that were on the road; for example, someone's house or a huge palm that could be seen from afar, they would indicate we were traveling in the right direction.

Although, to my fortune, Charif's uncles knew the

way well and that would ensure us to arrive without mishaps.

Twelve hours later we arrived exhausted and hungry, even though we had stopped to eat during the journey. Having gone with the uncles offered us the opportunity to get to know the area and its customs in greater detail, they traveled once a year and stayed there for a period of time, because they have to do the complicated task of counting wild cattle; a work that, due to the long extension of the land, which was about ten thousand hectares, required that it be done on horseback or in all-terrain trucks.

The house was simple, it only had one bedroom and a space from which several hammocks hung; nothing new for me, because in Guatemala we also use hammocks; however, what really seemed to me as a novelty was to spend the night in that immense sea of land in the middle of nowhere.

The aunt warned us it was the safest way to sleep to avoid the bite of any snake or poisonous creeping bug was to sleep in the hammocks. When I heard that, I almost died. That warning made me fill with fear, because although I was born in a tropical country, I did not know the fauna of the Colombian plains. However, I felt like an adventurer, and as always, I celebrated my great feat.

Further ahead it was Juaco's house, the foreman who lived there with his wife; they, among other tasks, collected the water that abounded in the natural pipes, which were underground currents that came to the surface and form a stream that, over time, sprouts on other sides. In those natural pipes there are beautiful little goldfish that are desired in many parts of the world, for example, in Japan; a country in which its residents appreciated them for their great beauty and ornamental function. One morning we took a bath in one of those water pipes. It was very pleasant, until Juaco warned us that we should not bathe around five in the afternoon, because at that time the piranhas were abundant, they arrived motivated by the reflection of the sunset over the water, in a threatening journey. When I heard that story, I was scared, but, in amazement, I also thought I was in a mystical place, unique in the whole world. After that, I knew the plain was the kingdom of the anaconda and the boas. I didn't want to meet an animal like that because I have a phobia for reptiles; however, that same morning, when we went to the pipe, not far from the house, I told Charif to observe a huge and strange leafless piece of trunk that was right on the road where we were going to pass. As we approached, we found that it was not a trunk, but a huge boa, which surely had just swallowed its prey, because it was distended in a part of its frightening body.

Because of my aversion to snakes, Charif worried about covering my eyes and calmed me down, making sure that because the snake was digesting it, it wouldn't hurt us. That was the biggest animal I had ever seen in my life, because, even when it was rolled, you could perceive that it was monstrously immense.

I turned pale. I couldn't tolerate being near those reptiles. I almost fainted, I even felt nauseous. Everyone laughed and assured me that this type of discovery on the plain was very common and there were so many species of animals that lived there, I could not know them all, much less familiarize with them. I tried to recover from the impact and continued to enjoy my stay in that place. Upon arriving, we prepare dinner. Juaco helped us to do it because that day he had gone hunting and captured a *chigüiro* or *chigüire*, which is a huge rodent, perhaps, the largest on earth, whose meat is much desired in the Colombian and Venezuelan plains. I would not participate in that feast. I didn't like the idea of chewing a rodent; I would only eat the garnish, a wild *yucca,* which was a plant that grew all over as if it were weeds. The same happened with corn, which germinated without anyone planting it.

We had dinner accompanied by *Juaco*; this gentle settler was a very special *Llanero*. He was small, but strong; without a drop of fat in his body, due to his active work. His skin was roasted by the sun. He was a true Colombian cowboy.

Of the most important attractions on the plains, and that I had the opportunity to appreciate during my short stay, was the *coleo*, a sport in which the rider comes out on his horse and grabs the animal by the tail, throwing it on the ground as to take it to the stable, bathe it, and deworm it. Those who practiced this sport, must have a lot of physical strength and must be trained to deal with wild cattle.

The dawn on the plain is glorious. To bathe ourselves with fresh water, we had to help ourselves with a *totumo*, which was bowl made of a plant that grew in the plains, and it was also used as a kitchen implement. Its equivalent in Guatemala, was the well-known *morro*. This is like a primitive *guacal (bowl)* which retains water or any other liquid, such as *Guarapo*: a fermented beverage, made from pineapple or sugarcane that is consumed in many parts of Colombia, and *llaneros* always carry with them to cool off during the arduous days of work and to give them strength to resist the inclement rays of the sun.

One morning we accompanied the uncles to rebuild the stable in which the wild cattle are kept, which, due to their wilderness condition, ends up shattering and destroying everything around them.

The cattle are housed in the *trinche* or trench, a narrow corridor, so the animals cannot move, and in this way, it facilitates the people the work, those who are responsible for feeding, bathing and curing them. However, despite the narrowness in which the cattle are, there are always a few of them that manage to jump or kick what's around them; they are completely wild.

In my tour through the remote areas of the plain, I never saw churches or anything like similar. In addition, I noticed the locals do not search for medical or veterinary services, they solve everything with ancestral knowledge they channel them through magic and witchcraft.

It is the sorcerers *llaneros* who care for the welfare of all: animals and humans. That culture, in the depths of the plains, was always beyond the reach of my understanding. The only thing true for me is that the magic of the Colombian plain hypnotizes.

To those who inhabit the indigenous reserves, magic serves to communicate with nature, with mother earth. What an envy! That is amazing. They are evolved communities.

Legends are many; for example, the locals claimed that people who penetrate the depths of the plain, when they want to leave, they cannot do so for they are invaded by a deep melancholy that makes them cry inconsolably until it weakens them. It is as if there was something invisible that would not let them go.

Undoubtedly, the most beautiful scenes I could appreciated during my time in the Colombian eastern plains, were the sunsets. It is the moment in which a huge red sun, cautious, is set aside to give pass to a flirtatious moon that shines brightly across the sky.

In the natural pipes, meanwhile, all kinds of birds converge; herons, macaws, hawks freely undertake their flight over that greenery; and colonies of *chigüiros* flee, to hide somewhere so as not to be engulfed by anacondas or the largest predator of all: man.

Every day we went out, in order to get our food, to fish or hunt *chigüiros*, ducks or other kinds of birds, or whatever moved, because to my disgust, also the meat of snakes is used for human consumption; I could never taste it. It disgusted me.

On the other hand, I was fascinated by the veal to the *llanera* style, it is the typical dish *par excellence* of the region, it is also called "*mamona*". It is succulent, and tender. And Its way of cooking is very particular: the meat, previously marinated with salt, is embedded in large sticks that form a cone, which is then located near the burning charcoals so that, little by little, the action of heat cooks it, to a strategically calculated distance.

A rainy morning the tractor broke down. Uncle Gerardo had to undertake, along with one of his workers, a three-hour trip to get to a friend's house and find the spare part needed to repair it. We all stayed at home that day because the weather didn't allow us to go out. Juaco and his wife accompanied us.

Time passed and uncle Gerardo did not return. We were worried. There was no way to communicate with him, since mobile phones had no signal.

Around seven o'clock at night, we saw a light in the distance; We calmed down because we thought it was uncle Gerardo's car. We started joking and speculating about the time he would take to get home. However, we noticed that as the vehicle approached, only a single light was on.

That made us laugh because we thought the car had blown a headlight; but then, and after observing very carefully, we noticed that in reality that light did not seem to be what we believed, because it came at a rare speed and seemed to trace strange movements. That, perhaps, was something else.

Gradually the light was approaching us. Its shape was round and large. Suddenly, it started jumping as if it were a beach ball. The closer it approached and touched the ground, the more it bounced.

We were fascinated. We did not know what we were seeing. We also had no idea how to act; stepping away, hiding or staying to see what happened were some of the options.

The closer it got, the faster it moved; that made us panic, especially when we saw that it was possible for that large sphere to hit the house.

Juaco, who had lived in that region all his life, was speechless; he assured us that he had never seen anything like that. But he did say that in the area there was a famous legend about *the Fireball* (bola de fuego) apparently, it was the same ball that our eyes were seeing.

We were all very scared. There was fear in the environment. Juaco, Charif, aunt Lucy, and I were waiting for *the Fireball* to approach. Juaco's wife ran scared to hide, as Charif's cousins did.

The strange sphere was approximately four meters in diameter. When it got to where we were, it didn't crash into the house, but it did pass very close. We decided, then, to follow it; but as we approached, it became blurring, leaving a phosphorescent trail in its way. All the path shone like minuscules stars.

The villagers could not believe it. They were scared, but at the same time pleased, the legend of *The Fireball* had come alive and they had witnessed that. It was a great event.

Shortly before returning to Bogotá, something happened that shook me and made me reflect on the little power of man. If I had not been a spectator of that event, I would never have thought that something like this could happen.

One afternoon, Juaco commented that he had to deworm cattle and take out the *nuches*, which were larvae under into the skin of animals, in the style of ticks and worms.

Perhaps because of this condition, some cattle had become ill, and as usual in the plain, instead of looking for a veterinarian, they went to a sorcerer, who would be in charge of curing the animals.

The infected cattle were locked in the stable, when that man arrived; a *llanero* that, due to the effects of the sun's rays, had a very dry and cracked skin. He dressed like most of the countrymen in the plains: shirt and white pants, espadrilles and hat; he wore a canteen or *totumo* with *Guarapo*. His platinum white hair suggested that the years had inherited him enough wisdom to do the job. Also, he was safely carrying tobacco, the most important tool to fulfill his mission.

We looked at him with curiosity. He suddenly expressed that he would "pray the cattle".

——Pray the cattle?

I asked Charif, who answered me with a: *Shhhhh…* An imminent order for me to be silent.

That man lit the tobacco, and slowly, began to expel puffs of smoke, and then to pronounce something indecipherable. A few minutes later, we began to see strange parasites coming out of the leather of cattle.

When the livestock was released from those abusive bugs, the healer sprayed them with creolin to disinfect and heal the wounds.

Among the cattle was a cow that was dying. Its eyes orbits were blank because of the deep pain it felt. The man stood in front it and after making his plea, the animal stood up as if he had never fallen ill. For me those events had no explanation; None of that I could understand.

With all these experiences I learned that, besides God, those creatures, called *llaneros,* could also heal the evil of men and animals. Unfortunately, during that trip, and in the most unexpected way, mourning came to our family.

One night that aunt Lucy could not sleep, she heard a ceremonial chant from a group of people. She thought that the strange chords came from a reserve of indigenous *llaneros* which was relatively close. Driven by curiosity, she peeked out the window and saw men who, with torches and candles, walked around an inert body that lay on an improvised coffin, a bed made of dry branches, while intoning a kind of requiem.

Something strange was occurring, however, she went back to bed. The next day she told us what she had seen. The settlers looked at each other in amazement and told her this was impossible, because the reserve was very far from the house and its inhabitants were unlikely to pass through there, with a deceased, late at night. They suggested it had been a dream. She insisted on what she had heard and seen. Then, Juaco and his wife, without euphemisms, told her this was a bad omen and the family would soon mourn. Someone was going to die.

That same day, uncle Gerardo fell off his horse and hit his elbow with a rock. A huge bruise formed over the hours. We thought it was best to go to the nearest town as soon as possible, for a doctor to check on him. While the doctors checked on him, he suffered a severe heart attack that killed him instantly. The premonition of Juaco and his wife had been fulfilled. Aunt Lucy was out of control. Her children were disconsolate.

After doing everything necessary to transfer of the body, we left the plains with great pain in the heart, trusting God would allow us to get well to Bogotá. And although our wedding would be spoiled by sadness, we knew that uncle Gerardo, from where he was, would be happy for us, and accompany us in spirit. He was an excellent man, a fighter and a great *connoisseur* of the plain; land which had finally stayed with our uncle. So much mystery hides that place ...

***

In Colombia, for more than five decades, the *guerrilla* of the Revolutionary Armed Forces of Colombia (Farc) intimidated millions of Colombians. This was a terrorist group that claimed to fight for political and social changes. It originated in a Marxist-Leninist inspired communist *guerrilla*, with which for many years the different governments faced each other throughout the country. It was a war that seemed endless.

By the time I lived in Colombia, the country was under the mandate of Álvaro Uribe Vélez, who for his persistent fight against terrorism, was reelected by Colombians for another period of government. At that time, the conflict had been about fifty years old and so far, no agreement had been reached.

That *guerrillas*, to keep up their struggle, kidnapped civilians and trafficked with drugs, among other illegal actions. The Colombian people suffered in their own land a merciless war.

This revolutionary group started there in 1964 with 48 farmers who inhabited the *Marquetalia* region, a small agricultural territory in the department of Tolima, in the center-west of the country. The founders were Pedro Antonio Marín Marín, aka Manuel Marulanda Vélez or Tirofijo; and Luis Alberto Morantes Jaimes, also known as Jacobo Arenas.

At that time, I wanted to enjoy my stay in Colombia to the fullest, that's why I dreamed of getting to know every corner of that beautiful country, but the armed conflict made it difficult for tourists to travel on Colombian roads.

Regardless of the difficult situation that Colombia was going through, we prefer to believe that we would not take risks and hope for what the future held with optimism, thinking that one day the FARC would make peace with the State.

When we leave Guatemala, you we were hoping to start a new life; now we were in a country where there was no peace; something that, perhaps, generates more destruction than an earthquake. Because terrorism and corruption, like a huge octopus, grab with its tentacles to men of laws, representatives of the people, authorities, and end the hopes of the population. The reality is that we were there and we would stay with our whole family in Bogotá.

Frightened people tried to follow their lives normally. We were about to get married; and in spite of what might happen, the date was approaching amid political and social conflicts; even so, we decided not to postpone it. Charif was excited and our whole family looked forward to the joyful event.

The day arrived, but with black clouds. The night I got married, the *Bogotanos* mourned hundreds of families: an explosive device of great power had exploded in one of the most elegant and important clubs in Bogotá. There were large numbers of dead and wounded.

***

At half past six in the afternoon, at Charif's house, everyone ran from one place to another with a joy impregnated with nerves, especially me, who was the protagonist of that story. I looked in the mirror and felt rejuvenated. The dress fit me perfectly. My sisters-in-law looked elegant, also my mother-in-law, who couldn't hide her excitement. It was the typical scene of a wedding that is about to begin.

When we arrived at the club, we had to wait outside of the room for a while, because although the guests were already inside waiting for us, the protocol of the *Zaffe* celebration indicated that we should appeared when the time came.

Behind the scenes we laughed as if we were a couple of silly teenagers hiding in some mischief.

The rumbling of some drums and the notes of a clarinet, which seemed to speak, were the key to indicate everything was arranged and the time had come to enter and parade on the carpet which was located in the center of the place and in the midst of men who, with solemnity, had made for us a street of honor, dressed in typical Lebanese costumes, beautifully adorned with white thread and rhinestones.

The sound of the drums and the clarinet was matched with that of Arabic flutes and tambourines. Once we reached the track, a group of dancers, with spears in their hands, surrounded us dancing the *Dabke*; a Lebanese folk dance. In their manly movement, the men jumped around us, stomping to the beat of the drums. Then, oriental performers known as the *belly dancers*, entered the scene and asked us to follow them with their sensual well-paced movement of hips. While they danced, we went to each table to greet the guests.

When this show concluded, typical of the Lebanese culture, Charif and I inaugurated the dance by bringing our bodies together to the rhythm of a romantic melody: "*Como fue*" a Latin *bolero*.

My arms surrounded his neck, his arms my waist, and rapt by love's spell, as if no one was watching us, our lips melted into a long kiss, while the guests clapped excitedly.

Once our participation ended, everyone went out to dance. The ceremony and the Arab reception were over, everything was new to me, and so wonderful, that I would never forget that day.

After a moment the celebration changed to the Colombian style. A group of musicians stormed the atmosphere with *Cumbias, Llanera* music, *Salsa* and other rhythms of the country. There was a table arranged with Lebanese dishes and, another, with Colombian delights.

Having married in a celebration in which the two cultures came together, it was very exciting for me. My family was wonderful and wanted, at all times, to make me feel like one more member of their family.

The party lasted until dawn. There I knew Colombians are very happy people. Already married, we left the club, with the dream in our heads of visiting Lebanon to find out the history of the Abosaid grandparents and tell it to the whole world. That was a fantasy that wouldn't come out of my head, until I see myself on the plane that would take us to that exotic and distant land.

FOURTH PART

"Being a boy, he killed the giant and erased the disgrace of the people. He turned the sling with his hand, and shattered Goliath's pride."

Ecclesiastical 47:4

The wait became eternal. I wanted to be on board the plane it would take us to live a great adventure; We would go first to Paris and from there we would take the flight to get to Beirut, at night.

The day before the trip, my mother-in-law was nervous, she told us it was not a good idea to go so far, and, less of all, to a country it had always been at war, because the *Hezbollah* organization remained in frank struggle against the Israelis in the north of the national territory, a region where almost one million civilians resided.

To calm her down, we promised we will not go near the borders; our trip would be to the capital of Lebanon: Beirut, and to some places of tourist interest, such as the *Baissour* region, which was also the goal and final destination of the trip. There, we would search for people who could have met Antonio and María Abosaid. Once we had the information we needed, we would return safely to Colombia.

Everyone understood my curiosity; they also knew we were risking ourselves visiting Lebanon. But my madness was so great that no one in this world could have convinced me otherwise.

We left for Lebanon on July 9, 2006. We took the necessary things. At the travel agency they recommended a hotel in the city center, located on *Hamra* street.

When we saw the pictures, we thought it was nice, it had good rates; they also told us it was situated in the heart of Beirut and the rooms had a spectacular view of the Mediterranean Sea.

***

The long-awaited day had arrived. We left for France on a direct flight and arrived the next morning. Already in Paris, while we were waiting for the flight to Beirut, I started writing a diary:

July 9, 2006

I am happy to be the wife of the "last Lebanese," as he calls himself. We are starting our honeymoon. We are going straight to find Charif's roots. I am very excited about that.

The flight attendant has passed offering beverages, we thought it would not be a bad idea to drink a glass of wine to toast for our new life.

After taking more than one, we enter in a kind of lethargy. Charif does not want to interrupt his reading about the country we are going to visit, even though his eyes are almost closing. He has read there are many interesting places we should visit before embarking ourselves on the search for the history of his grandparents.

Charif closed the little book and seriously instructed me by saying:

—Lebanon, Vera, is a very small country; you can see everything in three hours. Did you know that? he also said:

—Ah! You must remind me when we arrive at the

airport, we have to change the dollars we bring for Lebanese pounds, which is the local currency —he added—. However, they have advised me to pay with dollars, they accept them everywhere and the rate change can be convenient for us. We will decide there what to do. For now, we have about four hours to go, meanwhile, let's get some sleep —he said—, closing his eyes to try to rest. In the meantime, I continued with my diary:

The Paris-Beirut flight is going well. So far, we have not felt any turbulence. I have seen some women wearing "hijabs"; which is the handkerchief the Muslims wear to cover their hair and chest; others are dressed as Europeans. I have not seen many tourists.

It is time for me to close my eyes, but not before giving a kiss to my Charif, who seems absent from this planet.

—Until later, my love —I whispered in her ear.

Charif woke me up, pulling my hair gently, as a joke. He told me the pilot had announced that in twenty minutes we will be landing and we should remain seated. I took advantage of those last minutes to write on my diary:

The plane is full of children who cry without stopping, their mothers are desperate because they do not know what to do to reassure them everything is all right. We are flying over Lebanon; I am excited to see the Mediterranean Sea. I want to go to visit everything: The Roman ruins, the ski resort sites. Also, live Beirut at night, it must be different from the ones I already know. I want to taste its cuisine, see the famous cedars of Lebanon; the ash trees, cypresses and junipers, too.

Tradition tells that God planted the cedars in Lebanon. Its name: Lubnan, means "the country of whiteness", for its high snowy peaks. Charif says the word Lebanon means "white mountain."

I noticed he is very well documented. I love the little I know about Lebanon, and what can be seen from the plane will be nothing compared to reality, even though I also know we have reached a country in conflict ... I hope everything goes well, and if not, it will be part of the adventure.

When we were about to land, I set aside my pen and my notebook. I was overwhelmed by curiosity, I wanted to know what was in that legendary and mysterious land.

Already at the hotel, which, by the way, was not bad at all, and before leaving to visit the city, I sat down to write my first impressions of Beirut, after getting off the plane at *Rafic Hariri* airport.

As soon as we got off the plane, I saw all kinds of military vehicles and a contingent of soldiers with AK-4 rifles who were guarding the air terminal of any threat.

Customs officials were friendly when we presented our passports in migration. We had no difficulty with the language because they speak French, although with a strong Arabic accent.

They asked us if we came from Israel. We were seriously warned that if they found any entry stamp from that country, we could not enter Lebanon. We didn't worry about that, our passports clearly said we were coming from Colombia and Paris. After scrutinizing our documents to the last page and reviewing ourselves from head to toe, they welcomed us by saying: "Welcome to Lebanon," and with a blow, the officer stamped them.

Then, we went to the window of a local bank, there we had to pay about $18 for a visa that gave us the right to remain in Lebanon for up to six months. They advised us to report to the Colombian embassy, but it gave us a bit of laziness and we decided to postpone it.

When we left the airport, dozens of taxi drivers fought among them to take us to the hotel, which was about nine kilometers from the airport. We had to bargain the rate; Charif said asking for a discount was common, and if we didn't do it, they would charge us more.

On the tour we saw many buildings damaged by the bombings. The walls had huge holes produced by the bullets. We had arrived in a country where the word peace did not exist.

My writing had to be interrupted, Charif asked me to suspend it because it was too late and we had to go eat something. I decided to follow it later. I put on a jacket because the weather was chilly.

We went to dinner at a simple place, flooded with a cozy aroma of spices and cinnamon. I could not believe I was testing my favorite dishes. Charif was like a restless and hungry child. That night we had *hummus* dinner, *pita* bread with giant olives, *falafel*, *shawarma*, *baba ganoush* and *mammul* for dessert; also, other Arabic sweets wrapped in a puff pastry, filled with nuts and *pistachios*; Everything was exquisite.

My husband was in total ecstasy and immersed in a kind of trance for the satisfaction of the food, it made me think he had forgotten me. It also made me laugh, I kissed him on the cheek and reminded him I was present.

Then we went back to the hotel. *Hamra* street is a busy avenue full of pedestrians; we could see a good number of luxury cars, in addition to some ostentatious stores.

When we arrived at the hotel, we headed to the room. Fatigue beat us and we slept embraced; there was no energy for love. In the distance, an Arab melody was responsible for lulling us.

July 11, 2006

We have woken up with the call to the prayer or singing of the Adhan (aḏān) that Muslims do to summon the faithful.

Today we plan to visit the ruins of Baalbek, it is something we cannot miss. We will have to travel 86 kilometers from Beirut. We still don't know how to get there.

For now, we will take a shower and then go to breakfast. It's a sunny day, the weather is nice.

Charif, when he saw me half-naked, threw me a lascivious look; unfortunately, there is no time to make love, we can only think about hurrying to see how we will get to Baalbek. To calm his cravings, I promised him at night we will have a long session of love and sex, which doesn't have the same meaning. Love involves everything, sex for me, is the ultimate expression of love.

A taxi driver who recommended the hotel arrived for us. It is better to go with someone who has been well referenced, given that some drivers, with guns in hand, steal to passengers on their way. Its service, being particular, is more expensive, but it is more comfortable and safer than the public ones, which picks up passengers to cram vehicles, making the trip a hell. I must add the drivers of this country are reckless, there are no good signs on the streets, and these are full of holes.

From the car, in some parts, we saw a bit of greenery and the famous cedars of Lebanon. In the background we could see the snowy mountains. In Beirut you can go to the beach in the morning and to ski in the afternoon.

The driver, in an incipient French, announced that we were about to reach Baalbek. I have seen many Army controls on the road and yellow Hezbollah flags, in fact they say Baalbek is the territory of that group. That has made me somewhat nervous.

We, already are in the archeological sites. Hezbollah soldiers are heard on the loudspeakers, saying that they are "the Army of God", which, according to the taxi driver, are the ones in charge of this area. Without saying much and with a tourist book in hand, we calmly continue our journey.

For a moment, we wanted to return. It scared us when a man approached us to sell a T-shirt printed with the word of Hezbollah and the drawing of a rifle, which made me nervous. To avoid this, we pretended we did not understand what he said and with gestures we let him know that we no longer had money to buy it.

I have written these lines with great difficulty because the car has been in motion, but I had the urgent need to record everything that has happened so far on the trip. I hope to be able to decipher the story later, due that the writing is similar to scribbles.

We were back in Beirut almost at sundown. What I experienced that day would be recorded in my memory until the day of my death. I asked Charif to give me a couple of minutes to continue writing down my impressions.

We didn't go out that night. There was something more important to attend: it was love. I had promised my husband a night full of sex; so, I took a shower, and as tired as I was, I gave him all the pleasure that only a woman in love can give. He did the same with me. I will never forget that night because it was the first time, we loved each other into the enigmatic Beirut, and let ourselves be enveloped by the magic of the city. Despite the risk we were running, it was fascinating.

The magical moment concluded; we entangled our

bodies as if not wanting to separate them anymore.

The next day I woke up with an incredible desire to write. I grabbed the pen and my diary again and still in bed, I kept recording what we lived.

Charif never complained about my excessive desire to write, he just stayed by my side, watching me curiously, while I documented the trip to *Baalbek*. I saw a glow in his eyes, a guarantee he was pleased like no other, last night.

July 12, 2006

Despite the fear I felt on the way, I do not regret visiting those wonderful sites, I thanked the past, to the Phoenicians who built the temple of Bal, from which the city derived its name. The land through which extraordinary personalities had passed, such as Carlo Magno, the Romans and Constantine the Great, who ended paganism and instituted Christianity.

I was also stunned, from the entrance of the Propylaea, with the Temple of Jupiter, built by Julius Caesar; the largest building in the Roman Empire, of which there are only six magnificent columns left. I cannot fail to mention the temple of Bacchus or god of the wine, which was erected in the year 150 B. C. Walking through these ruins was an unforgettable experience.

Charif kept watching me without taking his eyes off me. I noticed that hot blood ran through his veins, from the way he looked at me, it was clear that he wanted more sex.

See you soon, dear diary, at this moment I have something more important to attend ——I thought.

After making love, we went to breakfast. That day we would visit some places, such as the avenue that borders the sea, called "the walk of the *Corniche*" and the clock tower at *Nejme* square. We would also go to see the *Mohamed Al-Amin* mosque, in front of the Maronite cathedral.

The night shone with a beautiful sky; it was crammed with tiny stars that presaged happiness. Full of energy we decided to go for a tour through Beirut.

Our first stop was in a cafe called *Raouche* rocks, its name is in honor of the two rocks that are placed in the sea, posing, as elegant ladies, to be admired.

In that area there is a wide gastronomic offer, and for that reason, there is a lot of night activity, hundreds of people arrive to visit the restaurants and many of them stay in the sumptuous hotels that are located in front of the beach. Beirut at night is a place full of joy and good vibes.

In the food you can see the French influence. The coffee places remain full; in one of them I tried, for the first time, the water pipe or *hookah*, with delicious aromatic tobacco. The Arabs like to stay out late and live the Beirut's nights.

I insisted to Charif I wanted to eat bak*l*ava, once I tasted it, I couldn't stop eating, it tasted like heaven.

The scented smoke of the *hookah*, the aroma of coffee and the unique spices of the east, grabbed my senses and my mind. Everything looked like a fantasy. A dream. I adored that culture.

We returned to the hotel, we needed to rest. The next day I wanted to see with my own eyes how refugees lived in Lebanon. Everyone advised me not to do it, because sometimes, without waiting for it, war conflicts in those areas are a threat, for they appear all of a sudden, but for me it was important to record those facts. When I told my plans to Charif, he said to me angrily I had gone mad, to which I replied:

—Yes, my love, only for you —adding a dose of coquetry with my words.

Hearing that, he turned to see me in disbelief. However, he closed the evening with a tender kiss. I responded to his kiss sensually and a few seconds later his Lebanese blood was boiling. His body started vibrating at the rhythm of pleasure. His Arab ancestry was revealed in the way he loved me: passionate and exotic; as it was Lebanon.

After making love and shortly before closing our eyes, the explosion of a bomb rumbled our room. An angry Charif asked me if I still continued with my absurd plan; with a kiss on the forehead I responded; yes. I would not change them for anything in the world. Then, he turned his back on me and said:

—Good evening —he murmured with antipathy.

After breakfast; a croissant and a cup of a delicious Arab coffee, we made our way to *Sidon*, where there were a good number of Syrian refugees.

I had to see what happened to people, so, when I returned to Colombia, I could do something for them, like organizing events to raise money to help the poor. Also, I thought that when I finished my book *The Last Lebanese*, I could donate part of my royalties to the cause.

We were about to leave the hotel when we began to hear bursts of submachine guns, airplanes flying over the city and bombs exploding somewhere; then, we realized that things were not going very well.

We turned on the television and the news announced terrible events, the presenter reported with aplomb —: *Three soldiers died when two armored vehicles of the Israeli*

Army, patrolling on the border with Lebanon, were ambushed by Hezbollah. There are three more injured, one of them is in a serious condition.

The journalist also reported that *Hezbollah* had two Jewish prisoners in his possession.

Then we read in the newspaper, information about a failed incursion by the Israeli Army into Lebanese territory, whose objective was to rescue their fellow prisoners. Similarly, the newspaper, reported the death of four soldiers of "*The Army of God*"; and the destruction of a *Merkava* combat car belonging to the forces of Israel, by the action of a powerful bomb put by *Hezbollah*; also, the death of an Israeli soldier who died in the attempt to rescue the bodies of his companions.

Everything that happened was a consequence of not achieving, through diplomatic channels for Israel the release of Lebanese prisoners. And having failed in the attempt, *Hezbollah*, had decided to bomb some settlements in northern Israel.

This was definitely bad news.

The war between Lebanon and Israel had broken out. Charif was worried and told me it was not wise to leave Lebanon; he thought it would be best to go to the Colombian embassy to see what they advise us. Upon arriving, there were people lining up, thank God, there weren't too many.

When we entered the office, the consul gave us a good reprimand for not having gone to report our presence in Lebanese territory.

The embassy had a list of some Colombian citizens who were going to be evacuated, of course, we were not on that list. However, they registered us, despite the disgust we caused them.

The consul recommended we return to the hotel, and not leave at all. The officials would contact you, by phone —he said.

However, I planned to ignore the instructions, I did not want to leave Lebanon without having the history of our Abosaid grandparents. When I expressed it to Charif, he stated to me:

—If I didn't love you so much, I would have left you. I think you're crazy, Vera —he added in a very bad mood.

July 13, 2006

The picture is discouraging. I feel guilty for having chosen this country to spend our honeymoon; In spite of this, I hope the bad days will not last long, because this side of the world has always been at war. It is a dispute generated for decades.

The atmosphere is tense. We have spent many hours in the dark, due to the bombing of Israeli planes. So, we decided to follow the instructions of the Colombian Embassy to not leave the hotel; I am taking advantage of the time to find out more about the conflict and to continue with my purpose of helping, in some way, the victims of the war. I also spend hours writing this diary.

News reports announced this was a war that did not respect the lives of civilians. The citizens suffered the disproportionate attack of the Israeli Government, since they were bombed in the places where they were concentrated. At the same time, this army bombarded offices, arms depots, arsenals, media and other infrastructure of the Hezbollah organization, including, the barracks located in the south of Beirut. Similarly, it flew bridges and destroyed roads. The airport had been attacked and was closed.

The news was all over the world; that's why we decided to call our family in Colombia to tell them that we were alive and they should not worry, that everything was going well; which was not true, but hearing our voices would give them peace of mind knowing that we were still alive. We dialed my mother-in-law's phone number and one of my sisters-in-law replied:

——Hello! Hello! ——Who is calling?

——I'm Charif——. I call to tell you that we are well, as soon as this is over, we will return to Colombia.

Then, a brief silence was heard and my mother-in-law's voice appeared:

——Son! What a relief to hear from you! You can't stay there, it's dangerous. Get out immediately! There's a war, that's what the media says here.

From one moment to another she busted into tears without being able to speak more.

——Mom... Mom! Don't worry, everything is fine here in the hotel; we think this will not last long. Be calm, I beg you. The news you hear in Colombia is worse than the reality we are living in. It's always like that. We will be communicating more often so that everyone is calm.

——Son, take care, don't go out——. Stay inside the hotel, please! God bless you ——said my mother-in-law in anguish.

Charif said goodbye, promising to call again as soon as he could.

***

Our plan to get information for the story of Charif's grandparents had been postponed; It was sad to recognize we would have to leave the investigation for a next trip, unless things returned to normal in the shortest possible time.

Seeing, we could not leave Beirut because of the war, the hotel granted us an economic rate, however, staying locked up was upsetting me; I wanted to go outside, but Charif stopped me with the threat of getting mad at me for the rest of his days.

The media reported that the civilian population who was in southern Lebanon was being attacked without mercy by the Israeli Army. A good number of civilians had already died, some of them were innocent children who had nothing to do with the cruel war.

I turned on the television and the presenter—with eyes filled with tears—, said:

—There is a crazy and wild bombing in the north and south of the country; the attacks are happening by land, sea, and air. The streets look desolated, destroyed, there are only ruins, burned cars, and there are no buildings or houses standing; Beirut looks like a ghost town. The sacred sites where the history of the world was born, *Baalbek*, *Byblos* and many other ancestral places, considered world heritage sites, are in danger of disappearing.

We were in the middle of a war that touched our soul for so much destruction and death. At that moment, I felt it was my duty to stay instead of fleeing, to see if I could do something on behalf of the grandparents to help the population, especially the children. At least, live the truth and tell the world through my own testimony, that is, if I survived the conflict.

July 19, 2006

Undoubtedly, the ones who are suffering the most are the poorest Shiite resident population in southern Lebanon, a large majority of Lebanese. I remember Gandhi's words: "An eye for an eye and the world will go blind." In a war everyone loses. While the great powers believe that Lebanon is a hotbed of terrorists, many in the world justify Israel bombing and killing civilians in retaliation for two abductees, and destroy this country by sowing death in every corner.

Hezbollah's reaction has been to defend its country; without this group, Lebanon could not have survived for two days. For its people, the members of this organization are their heroes, and his leader has impressive control among his troops: he has the morale of the fighters in the sky.

The time passed in between writing my diary and the cuddles with Charif. As I did not feel like writing, at that moment, I decided to dedicate myself to love, to surrender myself to love in times of war, remembering Gabo's famous novel: Love in the time of cholera.

I put aside my diary and with concupiscent air I approached Charif, who looked somewhat emaciated, not to mention he was tremendously stressed and scared; I kissed him, and he began to relax. Making love helped him draw a beautiful smile on his face. To make love, he always had a good disposition; my desire for him gave no interval either.

We get used to sleeping with the strident sound of submachine guns and bombs. We get used to be making love in the midst of tragedy. Among the sounds of death, you can love and also fall asleep. "Good evening, Lebanon, may God protect us." I thought, as I prepared to sleep hugging my adored husband.

July 25, 2006

Beirut is burning as the Roman Empire once did in Nero's time. I had not written again, I let myself win by the grief that this cruel war produces. We have been locked up for several days, frightened by the noise of the missiles, the bombs, the sirens of the ambulances, the cries of the wounded and the cries of those who pick up their dead.

I want to go on a tour to visit the affected areas, I want to be a direct witness of what is happening, to see everything with my own eyes and not through television.

I will try to interview some people who are on the street or in shelters. Beirut, every day, is filled with people fleeing the conflict in other areas of the country. Their views will be valuable.

Charif is always telling me that I'm crazy; I always listen to him as if it were a scratched record and I ignore his comments; however, this time I think he is right. He is warning me for my lack of responsibility when I go out in the middle of the danger, when the few times we have done it had been to go buy something of extreme necessity.

I have told him that he is not going to be a widower ahead of time, that I have more lives than a cat; I have survived an assassination attempt in Rome, an earthquake in Guatemala and the famous fireball in the Colombian plains. Ah! I forget to mention, I also survived the jaguar in the middle of the Petén jungle, which I later knew it was Don Chente's nagual.

When I think about this, I deduced that God wanted me to spend a long time on this planet; that is why I thought the war was not going to be an impediment to get the long-awaited story of our Abosaid grandparents, who, perhaps, were protecting us from heaven. Finally, Charif reluctantly agreed to leave; his only condition was: he would go with me.

Upon leaving the hotel, we could see a good number of people who were fleeing from the most difficult areas, places where Israel bombed from planes and attacked by land with Merkava tanks.

There is no cease-fire for their attacks, they drop bombs and missiles continuously. There is an Israeli battleship that is firing from the sea. The Israeli Army is sowing terror and killing hundreds of civilians. It is a hard punishment for the inhabitants of Lebanon. However, the news announces that Hezbollah is responding with improved tactics and strategies.

It is not known how this war will end. Israel believes it is fighting with a group of tiny capabilities, but, *Hezbollah*, in addition to being very well armed, has powerful projectiles to destroy Merkava tanks, which, according to the Israeli Army, are indestructible; nevertheless, the press affirms the opposite, assures they have already been demolished much more than one hundred.

During the trip I saw a large cellar with many children painting, I would have liked to visit them and contribute with my love to their precarious joy. Charif was sensitizing a little more, I felt him more united to me in the fight.

We were walking, when I saw in the crowd a girl who must have been 12 years old, she was playing as if nothing happened. I asked her name, in French, she answered me it was Aanisa; a Muslim name that means "virtuous heart." She had huge eyes, and on his face, a marked expression of sadness. She had arrived with her family to Beirut seeking refuge because the building in which they lived had been bombed; her parents had survived; unfortunately, not for long. I asked her about what happened, then, she commented:

"From one moment to another I was surrounded by corpses, including those of my parents," she told me so with a seriousness that frightened me.

She had been orphaned, and in addition, completely alone, until a family member came by her, he found her stuck on the rubble, paralyzed by fear.

We chatted for a while, saying goodbye, she hugged me sobbing, her tears wet my blouse.

While we were touring Beirut in ruins, I took pictures, but some soldiers came out and stopped me, ordering me to put away the camera immediately, then they told us:

——Where are you from? ——a military man asked, watching us from head to toe, and looking at the camera we were carrying.

I thought it was a good idea to show him my best smile and act naturally. I then replied, calmly:

——I'm from Guatemala and my husband is Colombian-Lebanese—— I responded without showing fear.

——And what the hell are you doing here, in the middle of this war?——he asked suspiciously.

——We just got married. We came to spend our honeymoon without imagining what would happen. Besides, my husband is of Lebanese origin, and we want to find out the past of his grandparents, who were from Lebanon.

——And what is that camera for? Why are you taking photos of this tragedy?

——We just want to record what has happened, we are good people and we have no political or military ties ——Charif told him with fear.

——But you should know that there are spies here that want to portray the situation to inform the enemy or to discredit our struggle.

——Yes, but we are not spying, we are survivors of the conflict, as you are ——I added.

——We'll find out soon ——said the soldier——, asking us to accompany him.

——You have to go through a brief interrogation for us to find out who you really are. Do you know anyone here in Lebanon?

——Not exactly, sir. We are staying in a hotel on *Hamra* street; the manager and the workers can tell you who we are.

——The spies are also staying in hotels ——the soldier said cleverly——. Come on, get in the vehicle ——he ordered them without asking any more questions.

Charif and I almost faint from fright, but we had to look good; nervousness could make them think we were guilty of something. I grabbed Charif's hand and squeezed it hard to cheer him up. His face was red and suddenly he went paled, he looked sick, I feared he might vomit. I tried at that time to convey him a little calm with my serene attitude. The journey was short. When we arrived the soldier asked us, with kindness, to get off the vehicle. Then we entered a small office where two officers were; in addition, there was a desk, a computer and two chairs. The soldier, without a word, indicated us with a gesture that we should sit down.

——Your passports, please ——he said seriously.

After scrutinizing them, he asked us for the camera and began to see the photographs we had taken. Without saying anything to us, he erased them all.

We were silent. We didn't move a finger, we seemed to be made of stone, than of flesh and bone. Once he finished his search, he said he would return in a few minutes.

That time seemed eternal, we were very afraid, we knew what happened with spies in such a fierce fight, surely, we would not have time to even say goodbye to each other. The man returned, when he entered, he told us:

——I've found out all about you. I called your respective embassies and it seems that everything is in order. You have nothing to fear. Can I offer you a cup of coffee?

——No, thank you very much. We just want to tell you we will not continue taking photographs and you can trust us; we are simply a newly married couple who wants to help as much as possible, remember my husband has Lebanese blood, we would never do anything against this wonderful country ——I said, trying to convince him.

——Well, said the soldier——, if that is so, I wish you a happy stay. I recommend you go back to the hotel, and if it possible, to stay in the shelter, because things have not been resolved yet.

——Yes, we will ——said Charif, with a better expression.

A few minutes before leaving, the soldier pronounced again:

——We are *Hezbollah* and we will defend our people by spilling every last drop of blood we might have left! My last advice is not to go around taking pictures ——he ended saying.

Before arriving at the hotel, we passed through the French embassy, and saw many people, who were piling up to enter, surely French and Lebanese-French citizens who wanted to be evacuated.

Some left the swarm with a disappointing expression, probably the ones who were not on the list, and had to be notified when it was time to leave.

Although it seemed contradictory, there were children bungling in the sea; in front of the *Corniche promenade* they were throwing themselves into the water and were enjoying, as if nothing was happening. I thought about the optimism and innocence that emanates in children, even in times of crisis.

After that scary adventure, we return directly to the hotel; perhaps, it would be better to spend the night in the air-raid shelter. We did not know if the fire would get worse later; the bombings continued non- stop. When we arrived at the hotel it was already dark. There was a dense dust coming out from the collapsed buildings, and it began to surround the place. The manager, when saw us, begged us to go to the shelter as soon as possible.

We went down with some tranquility. It was a small space; there was a wooden base, and on this, some thrown mattresses, a small refrigerator, an improvised kitchen and a TV that worked not too well. I managed to hear the presenter saying that the world was blind to the suffering of the Lebanese people, who felt abandoned. Then raw images appeared, they were corpses of children and adults scattered throughout the city.

There were also, children injured in hospitals trying to survive with serious damage to their bodies, mothers crying, men helping the wounded or digging through the rubble, trying to find their loved ones. Red Cross patrols with their deafening sirens were all over the streets. It was an apocalyptic and heartbreaking scenario.

When we arrived at the shelter there were four people who greeted us as if we knew each other before; one of them was called *Abbud,* who came from Tripoli. A place where there were also many refugees coming from the south, but, since the attacks had begun in northern

Lebanon, they had decided to leave.

Everyone tried to find a safer place; but, at that time, there was none in the country, all cities were being rammed and were risky.

In the shelter there was a very young girl named *Aamaal*, she was Palestinian and studied at the American University of Beirut. The reason she was there was because the study center was closed, and the building she lived in was quite damaged. She was Muslim and wore *Hijab*. She told us that her uncles resided in the United States, and at the moment, they were paying her expenses.

There was also an old man who caught my attention, his name was *Anwar*. He was the only one who did not speak French. He was accompanied by a middle-aged man who was his son: *Samir*.

We talked with pleasantness. It was not difficult to establish friendship, because we were joined in the suffering caused by war; Talking about what we felt helped us let off steam. They asked us about our origin. It was a valid question, because, who in their right mind would be living their honeymoon amid bombs and missiles. We told them that we came from South America. Then, they asked other questions, such as the reason for our permanence in the middle of the war. We, having nothing to hide, told them we had come to Lebanon to look for the story of Charif's ancestors and to spend our honeymoon, at the same time. When they heard that, they were surprised. *Samir* was very courteous when he learned we were foreigners; he offered us his help, anything we might need.

Something happened during the gathering that left Charif and me stunned. *Samir* served as an interpreter between his father and us, because he only spoke Arabic.

The young man translated into French what his father, between sobs, told us:

——Our house was partially destroyed. We could only get a few jewels and the money we had saved for an emergency.

——Specifically, where did you live in? Aamaal asked in a broken voice.

——On Mount Lebanon, in the village of Baissour ——*Samir* replied.

We interrupt the dialogue when we hear the word *Baissour*, and surprised, we asked:

——Did you know in Baissour a family named Abosaid? ——I asked *Samir* anxiously——. He nodded smiling; however, he addressed the question to his father, who replied:

——Yes, indeed, there was a large family baptized Abosaid, there are still a few members; I know that most of them emigrated to America, others live in Beirut ——said the old man; and added——: I remember Antonio Abosaid in his youth he was a great friend of my father, whose name was Hussein. I know he left for America when he was 16 years old. They maintained a solid friendship at a distance for a long time. They wrote to each other whenever possible; Antonio made my father aware of his life in the new continent through letters and some photographs I still have.

After that unusual response, I was so moved that I hugged old *Anwar*, Charif did the same; when we finished squeezing him, he looked at us curiously. Surprised, he asked his son why so much euphoria. We told *Samir* that Antonio Abosaid was Charif's grandfather and the reason for our trip was to inquire about his past, because we intended to write a book about the life of his grandparents.

—We'll take you to Baissour with pleasure —said *Samir*; I will also give you the letters that we keep, if you wish I will translate them, because they are written in Arabic —he told us pleased.

Anwar excitedly asked his son, once again, to translate him, and looking directly at Charif, he said:

—I understand that Antonio returned to Baissour seven years later, after his departure; it was when he met your grandmother Maria Simón and married her.

I could not believe it; we were so lucky. I was amazed, so I happily expressed to Charif:

—We won't have to go back. Now, we already know people so close to your grandparents, we can get to know their story and have the letters and photographs he sent. This is a miracle, my love! I said, holding him tight, pressing him against my chest.

He looked at me smiling. His eyes expressed tenderness and with emotion he replied:

—Yes, it's a miracle, Vera. Also, it's a miracle that we are still alive. You are very stubborn! When you put something in your head, there is no one who can take it out —he said complaining and joking at the same time.

While the others slept, we chatted peacefully with *Anwar* and *Samir*. Time fell short. *Anwar* referred to the Abosaid grandparents as good and hardworking people. He told us they had vineyards and fruit trees. He described grandfather Antonio like this:

—Antonio was a man of medium stature with a broad forehead, black hair and large brown-green eyes; a true Lebanese. The first time he traveled, he was destined for Mexico, he landed in Yucatán, because there lived an uncle who would give him a place to stay and work. He was an intrepid adventurer, a young man who wanted to know the world.

Although Mount Lebanon is very beautiful, my father always agreed with Antonio's departure, because the economic situation in our village was not well. We felt oppressed by the Turks and the Ottoman Empire. Wars between different religious beliefs made life difficult, we barely survived.

It was not easy to be under Turkish rule, because the members of the army arrived at our village in order to recruit young people to fight wars for them. The mothers were scared, some suffered the loss of their children on the battlefield; that is why, in the long run, they preferred they go away. Hence many emigrated —*Anwar* concluded.

It was dawn and nothing was heard anymore. There was a bit of tranquility, it wouldn't last long. We left the shelter begging not to be hit by some missile; before we said goodbye to everyone who accompanied us on that special night.

The hotel was partially damaged, but the bedrooms were still suitable for overnight stays. We were calm, maybe because we knew *Anwar* and his son would not go anywhere, they were also staying at the hotel. We were overwhelmed with a feeling of relief because we would soon get what we wanted so much: the story of our grandparents, I told Charif, with a wide smile.

That night we made the promise we would be together until the last day of our lives, and for no reason, we would give up on our dreams. We slept longing to awake free from the clutches of war. We had promised each other eternal and unconditional love; although, at that moment we realized how vulnerable we were, we didn't know if we could survive, because the war didn't seem to end.

My nerves are altered and my stomach began to show signs of acute gastritis. Charif also had his digestive system wrecked, because there was no set time to eat.

The city began to show the ravages of war: lack of energy, shortage of water and food. There were only two stores open, ironically one was a flower shop and the other a coffin factory.

We decided not to think about that uncertain future. It was better to disconnect from everything; to be depressed would not help with anything. We had to be braver than ever. Despite so much sacrifice, we already had something interesting to tell our family, and our love was growing more and more in the midst of adversity. Although the trip had many inconveniences, it had been worth it because in the end the war couldn't be an obstacle to end our dream.

August 4, 2006

We remain here as if misfortune were part of our daily life. Sometimes I go out to help the injured in hospitals, and take pictures with great care to show them to the world when I get to Colombia.

There is so much desolation. The faces of people show sadness, tiredness and despair. Today we have communicated, although with difficulty, with Mrs. Raquel, we have told her we are still alive, that she should not be alarmed, we have calmed her by saying everything is going more or less well. But it is a lie, the gas stations are closed, the fuel that is essential for power generation, and the water is running out. Humanitarian aid is limited, because the attacks prevent it from en-

tering. Everything becomes difficult. Every day is worse.

I accept I must have been crazy when I decided to stay and drag Charif to this dangerous adventure, if something happened to him, he would never forgive me. The news says that the majority of those affected are in the south, in the cities of Tire, Jezzine, Sidon and others whose names I don't remember well. Hundreds of them are living in public areas and in schools.

August 6, 2006

This is too much for me. I am very tense, but I will try to sleep a little, tomorrow I want to go to the Red Cross to help. I would like to go out more often, but the fear and the permanent explosion of bombs prevent me from doing so; for example, the missiles, which destroy anything they reach. In the confinement, at least, I take the opportunity to write.

At night we help ourselves with a flashlight to see, since there is no electricity. Maybe I will pray for all this ends soon; although my faith is weak; these situations make me doubt the existence of a God. I don't want to blaspheme, but, why if he is so powerful, allows children, elderly and many innocent people to die? If it's so omnipotent, why doesn't he do something to stop this massacre? I often ask myself these questions and I don't find answers. I know that HE will not come down from heaven to answer me, so I try to persist in my faith, and despite the anger that I have for so much injustice, I will pray. Forgive me, Lord, for what I am feeling! See you tomorrow, Lebanon. Goodnight My Love.

August 9, 2006

I don't have much to narrate this day. In war everything is bitterness, anguish, grief, hatred and lack of love among human beings. Now I have gone out to the Red Cross, I have been doing it all these days, I have heard sad stories and I have seen dead children; innocent faces that showed the cruelty of this war. I don't know how or where I got so much strength; it just emerged in this horrific and unjust conflict.

Doctors, amid a shortage of medicines, do what they can. The destruction of buildings leave dust everywhere; many of the buildings that have collapsed are hospitals. I try to be optimistic; I hope there will soon be a relative peace; however, what I see around me makes me think the end of such ferocity is far away.

During my visit to the Red Cross I met Hassan, a fourteen-year-old boy who was lying on a bed. His sad face moved me and made me approach him. I tried to caress him, but he turned his face; he didn't want to talk either. He was absent. I chose to express some affectionate words, while taking his hand in order to inculcate confidence; when I finally succeeded, in a precarious French he told me he had lost his whole family and several friends because of a bomb it fell on a funeral home where they were at that moment. He could not even bury his loved ones; their bodies had been torn apart and were left at the mercy of the dogs.

While narrating what happened, bitter tears slid down his dirty cheeks. His expression was of rage and pain. He approached me as if he wanted to seek comfort, he told me he did not want to continue living; however, he thanked me for being with him at that instant. I tried to convey a little peace and joy to him, and smiling, I took a bag of candy from my purse which I had managed to buy on the black market. He, with effort, smiled gently and put them under his pillow.

I also had the opportunity to learn about the moving story of Zaida, a girl with a withered and inexpressive face, despite her young age. The war had taken away all she had, her mother. A missile fell in the neighborhood in which they lived; his mother was alone at home, Zaida had gone out to buy the bread, this fact saved her.

—I do not have a father. Now I don't have a mother, or who to turn to when fear takes hold of me. I just want to die and go to paradise with her and with Allah —she added, rubbing his humid eyes, full of grief.

When I met Munira, an 18-year-old girl, her jaw was broken, which prevented her from speaking. She was a truly beautiful woman. She had huge electric blue eyes, her skin was cinnamon color, she had beautiful golden highlights which stood out, on a dark brown hair.

At first, she didn't want to talk to me, but I convinced her that by doing so, she would feel better if she told me what had happened to her:

—A missile fell on the roof of my house —she recalled with a lost gaze—. That caused a heavy block to jump off the roof and hit my face, causing me enormous damage.

There was horror and despair in her; but even so, her beauty had not disappeared. Amid such tragedy, Munira received good news: her face would be the same as before, there would be no scars left; only those of the soul, I thought to myself.

At that time, I would have liked to have enough money to be able to adopt all those boys, provide them with a home, and above all, much love. But it was nothing more than a dream, and although his tragedy hurt me deeply, I was aware that my hugs, my caresses and my encouraging words were nothing but palliative because their wounds were so deep, they would never heal...

Like those, there were several sad and shocking stories I knew and I don't want to keep telling, because I worry too much, when I remember the atrocities of which all those children and young people were victims.

I turned on the television with the false illusion of hearing the war was over; not finding something similar to what I expected made me nervous, so I was changing channels frantically, to see if anyone was reporting something positive, but unfortunately, it was not happening.

I decided to go to sleep, I felt I was fainting from sleep. I said good night to my husband. He approached me and gave me a tender kiss on the forehead, at the same time, he said:

——Goodnight my love; you don't know how much I admire you —— he whispered in my ear, and embraced me with tenderness.

August 11, 2006

It's been more than a month since the war began, finally, there is a mutual cessation of hostilities. Blessed be God! Although, there are still skirmishes near the borders, because both countries had broken the pact. However, we are on the verge of an absolute victory. Israel could not win Goliath against David; with all his might, he could not crush us. The triumph is due to Hezbollah and to its leader: Hassan Nasrallah.

People love him. He is the man of the moment in Lebanon. He has said the victory had been the work of God and it could not have been otherwise since the whole world saw it as impossible for Lebanon to win the war. Days of glory will come for the Lebanese people. Nasrallah has declared he will not leave remains on the ground, not a single rock; the Army of God will rebuild Lebanon. For the Lebanese, Muslims, Palestinian refugees, Syrians, Maronite Christians, Orthodox Catholics and the Druze minority, he is the envoy of God, the great defender of the people.

To think the Israeli offensive had killed thousands of people; injured more than three thousand, of which one third were children under twelve years old, and displaced almost a million, it was a real horror.

The governments of the countries which supported Lebanon always argued that the conflict had been initiated by Israel and their reasons were disproportionate; for that reason, and because the hostilities between Lebanon and Israel were very likely to continue, I thought it would be prudent to stay longer than expected. What else was there to do, we were still alive and the whole world had its eyes on Israel and Lebanon; longing that perhaps, the long-awaited peace would come definitively. In addition, we still had the task of compiling the story we had so longed for.

August 30, 2006

There is already peace, or at least, we are not being bombarded at all times. While the war lasted, I learned some words in Arabic. That has allowed me to greet, thank and expressed some very basic phrases.

Charif and I plan on staying until the end of September because we want to go to Baissour with Samir and Anwar. There we will have the opportunity to inquire more about the history of our Abosaid grandparents.

The hotel administration has passed us the bill and is quite high, despite the special rate granted to us; fortunately, we have enough money, Charif has some savings; that's why he agreed to stay here, besides, he wanted to please me, it was me who insisted. I will thank him all my life for so much sacrifice.

For now, this diary will close.

FIFTH PART

*"Take into account that true love does not know danger
or fear. Sometimes it takes you to live great risks. It survives
because it is perfect and strong as the root of a legendary tree."*

Anna Simon

The day was beautiful A radiant sun presaged happiness. The Lebanese were about to take to the streets to celebrate the great victory. Hundreds of thousands of people came to Beirut in buses, private cars or simply on a pilgrimage; they were proudly waving the *Hezbollah* flag. The crowd looked like the crest of a yellow giant wave which moved continuously. The jubilant supporters wished to see their top leader, *Hassan Nasrallah*. The voices of thousands of people were heard in unison singing proclamations full of joy.

Lebanon, regardless of its religious or political tendencies, was waiting for his appearance; he was like a God to them. The ovations of the mass increased when *Hassan Nasrallah* appeared.

Surrounded by his bodyguards they cordoned his body, forming a human shield in order to protect him with their own lives.

The man addressed his people saying it had been a historical, strategic, and religious experience to win the war.

With his arms raised and his voice firm, he said *Hezbollah* had fought led from the hand of God, and it had been a "divine victory" against the State of Israel. He also said he had decided to participate in that meeting, even though, his presence was a danger to him and to all his supporters, due to a possible Israeli attack. He continued with his strong and vividly speech:

——No Army in the world can force us to leave our weapons, we will defend Lebanon, not only the Shiites, but also the Christians, Muslims, Sunnites, Orthodox Catholics and Druze; and all the population without any political or religious distinction. I promise our weapons will never be used within Lebanon or against our people——. A moment later the applause rumbled in the place.

The voices joined as an impassioned chorus, full of enthusiasm, cheering their leader. Tears appeared on the faces of crippled people, of followers who could not contain their emotion and of all those who in one way or another had been affected by war. The streets and periphery of Beirut were flooded with supporters; the yellow flags stood out moving to the beat of the hymn of *Hezbollah -YA Aba Abdillah,* which the crowd chanted with one incomparable patriotism.

Women with children in their arms, elders and youth were there united in brotherhood.

It was an unprecedented It victory; something never seen by a world who kept silent and indifferent in the face of the slaughter, and the complicity of some Arab countries, ignoring the pain of his own brothers. The war was over and the victory parade was the proof of triumph.

***

It was difficult to get to the hotel, the swarm which

was everywhere, prevented us to walk. We wanted to get to the hotel to rest, and to place up our thoughts in order. The next day we would meet *Samir* and *Anwar* in the hotel lobby; they would take us to *Baissour*, we would be their guest for one week.

To go to Mount Lebanon was the prize from all we had gone through on our trip to Lebanon. After having risked our lives, we were finally going to know the land of Antonio and Maria Abosaid. We both felt an indescribable emotion knowing we would finally know from first hand, the story of Charif's grandparents.

After a good rest I woke up with more energy, it was a new day and the fear had dissipated. The bad times were part of the past, what happened was one more story to tell. We came down from our room and met with *Samir* and *Anwar*, who greeted us with a big smile. They were ready to take us to Baissour in his car. An old Toyota, which seemed to work perfectly.

We left Beirut, and on the way to Mount Lebanon, *Samir* informed us we would arrive in 45 minutes. During the journey we saw a sad landscape, ruled by destruction, in which, paradoxically, it was under a clear blue sky; perhaps, a contradiction of nature, a sign that a new era had arrived for all the inhabitants of Lebanon. After ascending almost 2460 feet above sea level, between narrow and winding streets, we arrive at our destination. Again, the emotion overwhelmed me, which made my mind and my senses played with me, making me perceive strange sensations, for as we entered the town, I felt the presence of the grandparents; I knew they were there waiting for us.

We arrived at *Samir's* and *Anwar's* house; which was located on a hill. *Samir* parked the car under a huge opulent old cedar tree that looked to not have suffered the ravages of war.

What was left of the house was only the living room, the kitchen and a bedroom, the rest were ruins. From above you could see an arid landscape, some greenery was barely seen between white rocks and rubble. The climate changed dramatically and we began to feel cold.

The house was made of white stone blocks, it had an *ajimez*, a type of arched window divided in the center by a *parteluz*, that is to say: a column. When we entered, there was a sofa and three large armchairs full of dust, like almost everything around. Likewise, a table, six chairs, a chimney full of ashes which showed it had not been used for a long time.

Samir and *Anwar* toured his house. The deterioration of the house made them almost cried; although, they swallowed their tears. *Samir* grabbed a piece of cloth and started dusting everything. I went for a broom; it was stationed in the back of the house in which there were two pines who seemed to take care of the place like silent witnesses of the conflict. As we started cleaning, a huge cloud of dust rose affecting our breathing and making us cough.

In the only room the war had left standing, *Samir* and *Anwar* would sleep. I would do it on the couch and Charif on the recliner. When we finished cleaning, we turned to see each other, and melancholy seized everyone, it was inevitable not to cry.

It simás hard to see a semi-destroyed home; even so, we calmed down, and thanked God the house could still be inhabited, and that we were still alive.

I gave one kiss to Charif. I valued his patience and understanding, it was all he could do. *Samir* went to where the bedside table was and opened the drawer to verify the letters and photographs would still be there.

We waited impatiently. It was the biggest treasure we had: the past of our grandparents.

After so much activity, we sat down in the living room to rest. Although the trip had run smoothly, we were really exhausted; a lot of adrenalin had run through our veins.

To dine we had bread and a jar with olives, which the hotel manager gave us before leaving. There was no more than that; the next day we would be going to town to buy groceries. The Lebanese are working people and I was sure they would be selling something. They wouldn't waste their time, and one of their great qualities was to know how to trade at any time and under any circumstances.

The cold was getting worse. We had to go find the few logs we had seen stacked behind the house to light the fireplace. Once the fire began to come alive, we perceived the warmth of a home, a dwelling semi-destroyed one which at that time housed its owners and a couple of guests.

We settled in front of the chimney, seated on the floor in a circle. *Samir* got up and, he headed towards the room, then he brought a dusty box filled with memories. Charif got up to receive it. I felt moved, my eyes were watery, filled with tears. I could not believe it; in our hands was the proof of the family past. Charif turned to look at me with admiration and thanked me.

The box was rectangular. It was made of rosewood; it had a flower formed with fantasy stones, and a mother pearl shell. Charif opened it with great care; inside there was a good number of letters. There were also photographs. Time and wars had not wreaked havoc on the grandparents past.

For many years those letters had been waiting to be rescued to let know that story. I was scared we couldn't get to read them, but when I opened the first one, I knew it would be possible. They were tied with a red and gold brocade lace. Shivering, Charif told me:

——Vera, here is what we have been looking; the reason for we have risked our lives. Now you can write the story of *The last Lebanese*. You deserve all my admiration; you are a strong and determined woman.

Addressing Charif, I replied:

——Now you will know with certainty what your grandparents did for you to be born. You owe them your life. They defined who you are now. I am so identified with this land and with your lineage, I feel as if I was born here ——I concluded.

Charif opened the first letter and gave it to *Samir* so he could read it, translating it into French; otherwise, we would not have been able to understand what it said. The text was addressed to Hussein, father of *Anwar*:

Dear Hussein:

I feel I am quite a man even though I am barely sixteen. When I arrived at the port of Beirut, there were many people waiting to leave Lebanon; some looked at me curiously. The journey would be an unforgettable experience, we boarded on the steam boat of the French line "Fabre". As I did not know what the route would be, I asked a sailor the name of our first port of arrival, and he told me it was going to be the port of Marseille, in the south of France, which would be the first destination and it seemed it would take less time to get there than I thought.

I was stunned by the colossal ocean which seemed end-less. I began to feel dizziness and wanted to vomit. Some boys who were nearby laughed at me when they saw me laying on the fence regurgitating. The movements of the boat from one side to the other, from up and down made me terribly sick. Although, by the second day my body had already got used to the sway.

I slept in a tiny cabin on the top part of a bunker bed, In the one below, there was a boy from Beirut who was complaining, and when he finally fell asleep, he snored like a lion. The food was very ugly; broths and boiled potatoes which had no taste. I used my food reserve. Do you remember I brought the copious meal Mom packed me, plus the jibs, olives and dried figs you gave me? Thanks to that I did not go hungry.

There were enough people on the ship, more young men than old; also, very few women, which I could count with the fingers of my hand.

I will write to you again when we arrive at the port of Marseille. There, I will have to stay for a few days. I will take the opportunity to visit Paris, I have heard wonders of that place, and of a famous high tower it seems to be guarding the city.

I have a mixture of feelings. Joy and sadness accompany me; I am happy because I will know other lands; and sad, because my family and you, my good friend, will be far away, which are the ones I really need. The adventure is just beginning.

With love:
Antonio

My dear brother Hussein:
We have arrived in Marseille. I still have some food ra-

tions: wheat muffins, some fig candy, dates, grape jelly and hard-boiled eggs. Our food is delicious! I do not know what I will find here, because the food I have will not last me the days I will have to wait to embark again.

They are saying the steamboat will take us to Cuba, and then to a peninsula called Yucatán in México, Uncle José is waiting for me there; it seems it will take us almost a month to get there.

Even though I'm not tired, and I have all the energy of a boy of my age, I don't know why I don't feel young.

Tell Mom, please, to order my brothers to collect the oak wood for the fireplace and to take the goats out. Also, the vineyards and fruit trees require care, you know it, more than anyone else. I miss Mom, it hurt me to leave her sad, with a broken heart, but my brothers and uncles will accompany her at all times. They promised me they will. In addition, I am in peace to know they are all very close so they would help each other. My father, may he rest in peace, would be proud to see how brave I am to undertake this journey.

Before leaving the ship, I heard the hoarse voice of a man who spoke in Arabic, but when I turned around I did not see anyone until his screams felt closer and closer to me, it was then when I could detect a man who shouted asking about the Lebanese who came from Beirut. He was a man who had boarded the vessel, for a moment. I thought I was dreaming, and I asked myself what was an Arab doing in Marseille? I could not believe it. The man, with a list in his hand, called by name and surname those who came from Beirut. People crowded around him. According to what he said, he was in charge of locating and guiding his countrymen in France, before the ship sailed out for America. Wonderful! I felt lucky. That evidenced patriotism and love for those of his land. All of us, Lebanese got off the ship. When we were on land, we formed a line and listened carefully to his instructions. One by one, we received some money, and some food. It was a miracle. Someone in a strange land was waiting for us. All I knew about the man he was known as the "Consul".

I thanked him for his generosity, he told me not to worry, for in each port there was a Lebanese willing to help his countrymen and the same would happen in Cuba, México or wherever we went. And then he seriously told me: ——You are not alone in the world; we Lebanese are everywhere. ——May saint Marón[1] go with you ——he said to me, giving me a strong handshake.

The port was busy. There were many grocery stores facing the sea. People walked along the pier, and the cafes and restaurants were packed. The French people dress elegant; some gentlemen wear tall hats; those of the ladies are decorated with cloth flowers. The atmosphere is cheerful. In my precarious French and through gestures I asked about the location of the train station, I want to go to Paris.

With love:
Antonio

Those letters kept so many stories, so many adventures, so much sincerity and courage, it was hard not to get excited. The history of the "Consul" did not surprise us, we knew the Lebanese are very united and supportive people who are always willing to help in good and bad times.

Charif, looked for the next letter and handed it to *Samir:*

Hussein:
I took the train from Marseille to Paris. The journey was not long. Next to me there was a pretty French girl, close

to nineteen years old. She was blonde, she had blue eyes and peach color skin. So much beauty overwhelmed me. It made me want to hug her and even kiss her. She smiled at me mischievously, it made me blush. I did not know how to act. You know I don't speak French, that's why I couldn't start a conversation; when we arrived in Paris, he expressed a brief Au Revoir (a goodbye). I said goodbye too, imitating her accent, saying the same words.

I had to find a place to spend the night. Everything is very expensive here. Fortunately, as I advanced on a large avenue, I saw a sign which said: Pension Phillipe. I was hoping they wouldn't reject me because of my status as an outsider. I was attended by an elderly couple, to whom I told I wanted a room. I showed them my passport and some of the money you gave me, they understood my wish and kindly let me pass.

The next day I went to Paris. I couldn't believe my eyes: a tower so high, that almost touched the sky; it is the emblem of the city, it is called Tour Eiffel. Not in a million years would I have imagined such a thing existed, with such a modern design. I was stunned. Paris is a city full of life. Its inhabitants walk through the wide avenues proudly. I took several pictures of this big city; I want also to become a good photographer.

Friend, I think I'm not so bad looking, some girls have winked at me. I wonder if all Parisians are this flirtatious. In our village the girls are quite reserved; apparently, here is quite the opposite. They say the city is in its greatest splendor, living in a moment which they call "Belle Époque". There are many cafes, cabarets and art galleries. Oh! I would like to return. I bet that from this city many artists will emerge, and will be famous.

I think in these days I will learn a lot in Paris, I like it so much I don't want to leave here, but I have to answer my uncle

José's call, the poor man awaits me in México with anxiety; he has always said his family is the most important thing for him, which is typical of a good Lebanese.

I don't know if I can write to you more; tomorrow I go to Marseille and I have to take the steamship it goes to the Caribbean that will take me to the Yucatán Peninsula. I have lived these two days with intensity.

As soon as I arrive, I will try to write you another letter to tell you how it was the trip on the ship. I miss you, friend; and I confess to you, even though I feel like a man, I'm still crying. Don't listen to me, I feel nostalgic for my mother, for the rest of my family and for my homeland.

Antonio.

It was enough. We didn't have more energy to hear more stories about this adventurous and daring young man. Maybe, he was like that, because Phoenician blood, who were travelers par excellence, ran through his veins; however, it gave to us a little sadness to know that when he left his land, he was only a child who was facing an unfamiliar world, without knowing what fate awaited him; the fact touched us.

We woke up tired. To know the history of our grandfathers was exciting, and at the same time exhausting, even though I was eager to hear more experiences of Antonio Abosaid.

After l breakfast, we went to the center of the village to buy food. It was a sunny day, but the cold wind cut the skin of our faces. We also went to church to thank saint Maron.

When we left the temple, we headed for home. *Anwar* would prepare lamb leg for dinner; he would faithfully follow an old recipe he jealously kept, and didn't share with anyone. Then we would continue reading the letters.

—¿Do you remember in what part of the story we are?—I asked Charif.

—In the trip from Marseille to Cuba—. He answered.

The night went on peacefully; it was too quiet that frightened us, because you never know what can happen in Lebanon, all of a sudden.

We sat in front of the stove, as we had done it the first time, and *Samir* opened the next envelope to continue Antonio's interesting story.

None of the letters had dates, but it didn't matter, we could always find out what happened since he left Lebanon, until he arrived at his destination.

Hussein:

I am in Cuba. If you had to go through on that furious and traitorous Atlantic, I think you would not want to come here. There was a horrible storm. We thought we were going to be shipwrecked.

Everything was going smoothly under the rays of a warm sun. There was little time left for the sun to hide behind the horizon, when all of a sudden, the wind intensified, and what had begun with a delicious breeze, became a threatening hurricane.

I was near the railing and I almost fell into the sea. The sailors ran desperate and urged everyone to return to their cabins. The sea was enraged. The ship was moving violently from top to bottom in such a way, breaking the waves with such force, I thought it would split in half. The sky turned black. Everything indicated the ship would sink into the im-

mensity of the sea. Screams of dread were heard. People piled up when they wanted to go down to their rooms, in search of a safer place or to locate their loved ones.

Unfortunately, in that confusion, two people died. An older man was pushed by the wind when he was trapped in the bow. The storm dragged him and made him fell into the furious ocean; the waves, which were giant, swallowed him in a second. The other fatal accident was of a nine-year-old boy, who recklessly, escaped from his father's hand and fell into the sea, in the face of the powerless gaze of his parents. His parents shouted for someone to save him, but it was too late, nobody could do anything.

I hid in the bottom of the steam and waited for the sea to calm down. I was horrified to think there would more tragedies.

I had never suffered so much, my dear friend. The anger of nature lasted throughout the night; the first rays of dawn showed a serene sea. Who would believe that calm ocean had been the murderer of the night before?

I saw some people who still reflected fear on their faces. Many were sad and even regretful of having embarked on this journey full of risks and uncertainty. I was convinced that, although the sea was beautiful, it had the devil in its entrails; but I wanted to be optimistic.

In the following days, the ocean showed no antipathy against us. That ship moved with grace and slowness, it seemed to slide over a sea of silk.

We arrived in Cuba at dawn. Several compatriots were received by family and friends. In the place was another man with a role similar to that of the Consul, the individual who held out his hand in Marseille; in Arabic, he called his countrymen by offering them work for those who wanted to be living on the island. For saint Marón! Hussein, we Lebanese are *all over the world. Is incredible.*

I will continue the trip, but first, I will spend a couple of days in Cuba, which is an earthly paradise. There is a lot of vegetation, green is everywhere, and very tall palm trees, very different from ours. This site is very unlike Baissour; the weather it's too hot, you feel your skin burns, but still, I like it.

Please, share these letters with Mom and all my family.

Fraternally:

Antonio

At the end of the story, Charif hugged me. His gaze was invaded by melancholy.

At that moment I missed his body, his love caressing my skin. The war snatched us many moments together, our honeymoon had been overshadowed by despair and uncertainty. Now that the conflict was over, and we were in a small space, I wanted him more than ever; but we lacked privacy. However, I knew that sooner or later we would have the opportunity to make love and to feel our bodies to burn with passion, more that the fire, which night after night warmed us.

The day it was destined for love finally arrived. *Anwar* and *Samir* went to visit relatives who lived far away. We took advantage of his absence and made love without limits. We had closed the windows and secured the door. Sitting on the couch, the fire in the fireplace sizzled and so did our hearts.

I stood up, and to slow down the agony of desire, I undressed little by little, looking at him with lust. He could not stand my look, and began kissing my breasts, squeezing them like a possessed. He touched my back with his hands, until he reached the birth of my buttocks. I leaned down and kissed his neck. I wanted to taste every inch of his skin; when I played with my tongue inside his ear, he started to moan of pleasure. Then my hand went down to his sex and as I touched it became so rigid, that I thought it was going to explode, he was ready for me. His body was mercifully asking to penetrate me.

His breathing was agitated, and his kisses turned my guts into a boiler about to blow up. His tongue played with mine. My excitement was at its fullest. We were burning of desire. He prevailed the need to merge into one. I felt I could not wait any more, I pulled away from him, and leaned back on the couch, I provoked him opening my legs to offer him the gift so longed for.

He kissed me uncontrollably from the tip of my feet to the point where he made me scream of pleasure. I felt the shake of his member inside of me, my body was pleased and relieved. After an intense orgasm, we stayed, entangling our legs; shortly thereafter, I went back to the sky, when once again I reached the climax, he at the same time, whispered a gentle: I love you, in my ear.

—Me too, with all the strength of my soul —I said, while looking at him with an expression filled with love.

The love affair ended among sighs and exhausted bodies. Charif transported me to paradise, as nobody had ever done it before. He tangled his fingers between my hair, and stroking my face he repeated: I love you. His face looked placid. His eyes shone happily. Then came the silence that comes after the pleasure. We kept silent staring to the ceiling of the room, thinking about how lucky we were.

At last, we had had time for us. I felt happy and I was sure happiness would last a lifetime. Time had passed quickly. When we realized it was later than we thought, we dressed in a hurry and went to town to get something to eat.

Anwar and *Samir* arrived very late; they told us their relatives were fine and it was a miracle they were alive; a missile had fallen near their home. *Anwar* asked us if there was something new, we looked at each other with mischief and complicity, trying to hide the obvious, since we had done something pleasant; which we couldn't disguise. Because of the expression in our faces, *Samir* understood, and smiling he asked his father not to be indiscreet. Old *Anwar* felt ashamed.

The next day we continue reading the letters. I was eager to know Antonio's experience in Cuba.

At night, as usual, we continue with the same routine. Nobody wanted to miss one single detail of the adventures of Antonio Abosaid which were becoming more interesting every time.

We brighten up the encounter with Arak; a liquor similar to brandy, of milky appearance, which is obtained by molasses distillation, fermented with a yeast extracted from the rice; It is native to southwestern Asia. After a toast, we were all ears.

My dear friend Hussein:
I've been to Cuba for ten days; It's very, very hot. An Arab man has traveled with me to whom people nicknamed him; "the Turk", although, he is of Lebanese origin. You know our passports are Turkish and that is why they catalog all of us as Turks. The people ignore we are Lebanese, but that is a matter of general culture, which few have. Although to tell you the truth, that does not bother me, since we all know that we are under Ottoman domination, and for the moment, we will not be able to separate from it. Someday Lebanon will be free and

everyone will call us Lebanese, even though I feel there is certain disapproval for our race.

The people here are cheerful and kind. Cuba is a country full of beautiful beaches, covered with white snow color sand. I don't understand anything they say. I have seen they drink a liquor called Rum, extracted from sugar cane, here there are large plantations and many locals work on farms under the intense sun. The persons here have African and mestizo origin; that's why some have white skin and clear eyes.

The color of the sea water is of different shades of blue and has violet stripes. When the breeze comes from the ocean, the heat does not feel so much.

The Turk took me to a lodging owned by a Cuban family. I rented a comfortable room and tried a wonderful meal: "bananas in rajas" (strips) and a well-prepared pork, I ate a good portion, since I am not Muslim.

Music is everywhere; groups of three or four people playing guitars and maracas which are hollow spheres with seeds inside, producing a rhythmic sound. Musicians are everywhere. People dance and sing, it is an island full of joy and festive musical notes.

The steam ship sails within two days. It will not take so long to get to Yucatán, according to what I have heard. There, my uncle José will be waiting for me.

I already feel better, even though I'm still far from home. Tell mom that I'm getting more used to it. I still don't speak Spanish, but I'll learn soon. Goodbye, Hussein. Greets to my family. I will write to you again when I arrive in Yucatán.

Receive a big hug:
Antonio

After reading that letter, we set out to dinner. During the meal we talked avidly about everything we had heard and left the table with more desire to continue hearing those stories.

We revived the fire with the poker, and put more wood. *Samir* opened another letter:

Hussein:

I felt welcome in Yucatan. Uncle José was accompanied by another Arab who, like in Marseille, and in Havana, received his countrymen to help them.

Some of those who come with me have names immigration agents find it difficult to pronounce, so, without even asking, they baptize them with a new one; sometimes they even change their last name. The poor without understanding what is going on, remain silent and speechless.

The Consul here has explained to me that this is done only in order to make the pronunciation of their names easier for others, also to make immigrants a less complicated life. For example, one whose name was Nasr was given Narciso; to another which had for last name Cadrehim, they have changed it to Cadre. To me, thank God, they didn't change my name, neither my last name. I would have felt offended! Thanks to my parents, my name is Antonio Abosaid, words that are not difficult to pronounce.

During the trip we did not suffer any mishap like the one we lived in the Atlantic. It seems the Caribbean Sea is calmer.

I am very happy to have met my uncle; he has been warm and kind to me.

After passing the inspection I was registered with my Turkish passport, and immediately afterward, we left for his house. Uncle José lives very well. It has a big house, it's all painted in white, the entrance has two tall palm trees. In the back there is a terrace with arched columns, and in front of it, a very large garden, full of fruit trees. On the terrace there are wooden and other furniture made in rattan. Uncle José taught me they were made of the wicker leaves of the thin branches of a shrub called willow, when folded, serve to form all kinds of things, such as baskets, furniture and other objects.

Everything seems interesting here. I want to take many pictures. The food is very spicy, but it tastes good. There is a dish called Cochinita Pibil, which is pork marinated with spices from the area. I love it!

As for my bedroom, Hussein, I can't ask for more. I have a thick mattress and a bathroom just for me. This is what I call "good living". Tomorrow I will start to work; as you know, it won't be difficult for me, since I've always been used to work hard.

PS: I have put a fan in front of my bed, and another huge one my bedside table. It's very hot here! As it was in Cuba. Regards.

Antonio

Charif, without waiting, opened the following letter and handed it to *Samir*:

Dear Hussein:

In Yucatan, most people wear white or light colors because the heat is very intense. As for the women, their white dresses are wide and adorned with brightly colored flowers; these garments are called "Huipil." Men wear fine straw hats that appear to be cool. So far, I have not worn any hat.

As for the language, I hardly understand one of three words. After two weeks I understood some, although basic, have helped me to communicate with the inhabitants of Yucatan.

I have gone to uncle José's store, he has shown me everything he sells; it has a variety of fabrics and haberdashery of all kinds: needles, lace, thimbles, ribbons, buttons, among many other curious articles.

Uncle José told me it took him a lot of work to create his store; he had to walk great distances to be able to sell his merchandise and thus raise enough money. He carried the merchandise from door to door, and since people could not pay it at once, he would left it to be paid into monthly installments; for that reason, he would walk through the streets with her backpack on his shoulder, and people when saw him would greet him with kindness, saying: there goes Joseph, the "abonero", (a person who sells to you on monthly payments) Over the years, he was able to open El Porvenir, which is the name of his warehouse.

Hussein, I'm already a worker at El Porvenir. I am proud to be part of my uncle's great effort. The days are long, but I am happy. I help myself with his gestures, like a mimo, to be able to sell in the store; I hope in a few more months I can make myself understand better. I send love to you and to all of mine, especially to mom.

I have missed them:
Antonio

We could not and did not want to stop reading the letters, so we continue with the following:

Dear Hussein:
Time flies. Several months have passed since I last sent you a letter. I know I have been a little ungrateful for not writing to you before, I beg your forgiveness, but I have enrolled in the Mexican Federal Army. I am fighting on the battle front, in a war that is not mine, but in which I have to fight for the welfare of the country which opened the doors for me. You know that I am a grateful man. Do not worry about me.

This fight has been called "The Caste War"; It has been

many years now. It is a social movement of the Mayan natives against the population of whites, Creoles and mestizos, dating from 1847. I cannot extend in the details, but I tell you the Mayan Indians fled to the jungle, people say they have founded villages there; its leaders have been abducted and executed by the Federal Army. I have to defend Yucatan from the rebels. I am pleased to have served Mexico in this matter.

Something curious and interesting happened. Among the soldiers I met a sergeant who participated in the firing squad of Maximilian, Emperor of Austria; before he was shot, he asked, as a last wish, not to be shot in the face. The Emperor, to ensure his longing would be fulfilled, took off his dumbbells and gave them to a sergeant. The surprising thing about all this is that he has given them to me, perhaps, because when he sees them, he feels guilty of being part of that firing squad. Now, I have a bit of the history of Mexico. The dumbbells are well locked in a closet in uncle José's house.

My uncle says I'm crazy, I think he's right; perhaps, it is not madness, but a fervent adventurous spirit. At this moment I am writing to you, I am already back in my work, and with what I was paid in the Army, I have bought a beautiful camera, I am thinking of portraying characters and going to events in my spare time to see if I earn a little more of money. I may be able to photograph President Porfirio Díaz himself. Why not. I know he is a man of character and ambitious, with a futuristic vision.

In this regard, I tell you, Hussein, that during the war I had an accident, I broke five ribs, and, under these conditions, I had to walk twelve many kilometers to the camp where I was. I do not regret that, because at that moment we were told that we would have the visit of President Porfirio Díaz. When I met him, he knew I was a foreigner fighting for his country, so he hugged me as if he had been a great friend, congratulated me on my courage and wanted to know my full name and address. I didn't understand why he needed that information of me. I thought he was a nice man. We create a friendly bond; so, I think I'll have the opportunity to take him a picture.

If it had not been for the help of the Federal Army, we would not have been able to defeat the rebel indigenous groups. That region in which they previously lived is now called the Federal Territory of Quintana Roo.

Tell Mom I already became a real man, and I want to return to Lebanon; I'm just hoping to save enough money to not arrive empty handed; besides, I want to return to my land and fall in love with it once more; the girls here, although they are very beautiful, are not to my liking, they are too liberal, though less than the Parisian girls, I have to admit.

Hugs:
Antonio

After reading these letters, *Anwar* told us about Antonio Abosaid's return and his brief stay.

When he came back from America everyone thought he would come with a lot of money, according to my father and relatives of Antonio, who expected to receive numerous gifts from America. Unfortunately, it wasn't like that, he carried money, but not so much, though he brought some gifts to friends and family.

Antonio came back to Baissour after being absent for almost seven years. He said that in addition to having fought against the Maya rebels, he had lived part of the Mexican Revolution, where he heard the name of *Pancho Villa* who was the leader of that revolution, and some others he didn't remember their names. He said the revolution had broken out in Mexico, when he served as president, Porfirio Díaz, a man appreciated by some and hated by others, even though he brought progress to Mexico. During his period, he told us there was a lot of disagreement in some citizens, especially in the peasants, because the owners of the large estates exploited them, and with the little money they earned , they had to buy the groceries in the stores of the *haciendas* whose prices were exorbitant which indebted the employees for a lifetime, without them having a chance to pay the debt. In short, their lives were the property of the landowners. It was almost like being slaves.

Antonio and the president of Mexico met, maintaining fluid communication.
They never dissolved that link, *Don Porfirio* admired Antonio for going to join the ranks of the Federal Army, despite its Lebanese origin.

Porfirio Díaz was considered by many, a dictator and oppressor. The Mexican people, mostly after thirty years, ended the mandate of Diaz with a strong insurgency. He died in Paris at age 84. During all that time Antonio and the former president maintained their friendship, to the point that when Antonio's first child was born, Porfirio Díaz sent him a congratulatory letter that I read, so I confirm it is true.

When listening to the stories of *Anwar*, we thought Antonio had gone to Mexico fleeing from the wars in his region, and to look for better opportunities to progress. However, and paradoxically, he had been fighting other people's wars. Maybe he had done it because he was an adventurer. He was an innate seeker of emotions; therefore, I was not surprised at his way to live in the distance.

I interrupted *Anwar* exposure to assess that Antonio Abosaid must had been a very charismatic and intelligent man, to have retained the admiration and friendship of a man like Porfirio Diaz. Then, *Samir* continued to translate what *Anwar* had to tell us:

—According to what my father once said, Antonio met Maria one afternoon when they gathered at the grandfather's house.

It is said María was a lovely young lady with clear skin, honey color eyes and silky hair. She had such fine features it seemed an artist had sculpted them with such perfection. When she met your grandfather, she was about 19 years old —he told Charif—. I know Antonio was captivated with her beauty, practically, they fell in love immediately. They were married here in Baissour, and their first daughter Josefina was born from that union.

Antonio decided to return to Cuba with his family, he would take a risk again to cross those restless seas looking for a better future for his family. He already-knew those lands and would not find it difficult to settle again. In addition, he recalled that in Cuba there were many Lebanese who had settled in the same year he traveled for the first time; and, while he was in Yucatán, his uncles Juana and Pedro had migrated to Havana, so he thought he could find support in them.

One day of April, Mary and Antonio, with their baby in arms, left Baissour forever. My father was very sad about their departure. Although the mail was more spaced, they always maintained contact.

Charif jumped and asked excitedly:

—More letters?! *Anwar*, do you mean there are more letters from grandfather after his second trip to Cuba? *Samir* nodded and went to bring the chest where they were kept. He immediately handed them to us. Charif, speechless, asked *Samir* to translate them.

Hussein:

We find ourselves very good. Juana and Pedro, my uncles, are happy for our presence here on the island. We have moved to eastern Cuba, to a place called "Puerto Padre". It is beautiful. It is surrounded by exotic beaches. This was the first place where Christopher Columbus landed. The locals say their name originated because one of the navigators, seeing the beauty of the landscape and its blue waters, exclaimed——: What a port, oh mighty God!

I am dedicating myself to photography. I am the official photographer of the Mayor of Puerto Padre; I also help the Mayor in whatever is necessary.

My life is quieter. I can no longer be so adventurous. Now I have my wife, two beautiful daughters and another baby on the way. My wife is a diamond and my girls, Josefina and Raquel, are more beautiful every day. Raquel, my Cuban girl, will be three years old; Feffa has four.

We send you a big hug, my dear friend.

Antonio, Maria and children.

The following letter read:

Hussein: I know it has been a long time. Life goes smoothly. When I am not working, I am with Maria and my children on the beach. The children are restless. They want to play all the time.

The family has grown. I have seven children: Pepe, Alberto, Miguel, Josefina, Raquel, Lucy and Luisa. Maria is a perfect wife; always attentive to everything we need in the house. She is patient and follows me where I am going with that sweetness so characteristic of her.

Unfortunately, not everything has been said. Raquel is affected by skin eczema. We have visited several doctors and have not found an effective cure. She is depressed, to the point that she does not go to school because she is ashamed.

In that effort and driven by despair, we turn to the natural medicine of the island; we visited a sorcerer known as "Aurelio el Chivito". Whoever recommended he, assured that he will end that painful disease.

This man lives in an unpleasant hut. Its appearance scares because he is deformed. It has a very large head and a small body. He is unable to walk, so he moves himself in a baby carriage. He always carries with him, as an amulet, a cross with semiprecious stones.

As soon as we arrived with Raquel, the man stared at her and proceeded to prepare a kind of ointment based on strange herbs. He rubbed the affected skin with that anointing and exposed her to the sun for twenty minutes. Miraculously Aurelio "el Chivito" cured our little girl.

I tell you this so you know there are many mysteries in Cuba. To cite an example, there is Santeria, a religion whose origin comes from the African Yoruba tribe.

As you will see, a healer sorcerer has been the only one able to heal my little daughter.

I conclude by telling you that Cuba is under the mandate of Gerardo Machado: "Water, roads and schools," is the motto of his government.

We send you a big hug, friend. Greet me, please, your family and the few left of mine.

Antonio, Maria and children.

Samir revealed to us that *Anwar* had more letters from Antonio, but because his memory was prodigious, he wouldn't need to read them; he would tell us what he had done the rest of his life.

He promised he would give the letters to us so we could keep them as treasure. *Samir* continued with his translator role saying ——: when Raquel turned fifteen, the political situation in Cuba was not going well, there was a great economic depression, it was becoming unbearable to stay in the island. When the Abosaid family decided to leave Cuba, Fulgencio Batista was in power.

It is worth mentioning that Antonio came very close to Freemasonry a secret fraternity, which has nothing to do with religion, it is a philanthropic, philosophical and symbolic institution.

During the meetings they didn't talk about religion or politics, its purpose was to promote the moral and intellectual progress. That activity never quarreled with his doctrine, for he believed faithfully in a supreme God, The Great Architect of the universe, according to Freemasonry. María would never attend the reunions because women were not admitted.

Antonio and his family left Cuba, thanks to a cousin of his, who was based in Colombia, she advised him to settle in Bogotá. She, in her letters promised to help him get ahead with his family in that country; she thought Antonio could work with his son Carlos in his warehouses.

Everything was going well for that family, the money was bubbling like spring water, and she thought her cousin Antonio could also drink from that source.

The trip became real. The Abosaid family traveled by train from *Puerto Padre* to Santiago de Cuba, and from there, they embarked to Kingston, Jamaica; to finally arrived in Barranquilla, the most important port Colombia had over the Atlantic Ocean, for it was called the Golden Gate.

Antonio left with his family. He took with him his most precious object, his camera and the hundreds of beautiful places he had captured through his lens.

They were full of enthusiasm and trusting in the help their cousin Abosaid would provide, but things would not be as easy as they thought.

SIXTH PART

"Who could be like the river, be runaway and eternal."
Sweet Maria Loynaz

When the Abosaid family boarded the steamboat to Barranquilla, it was a great event for their members. Large migratory groups entered the country through the Caribbean city of Barranquilla, and in order to reach Bogotá, they required to navigate across the Magdalena River.

Around this river were born all kinds of legends, like that of the man who had become an alligator. The Magdalena was not only an imposing river, it was also important for the development of the country of Colombia, because it facilitated the transport of people, animals and merchandise, also, because it provided food for many families who lived on its banks and surroundings.

Antonio, Maria, and none of their children had ever seen such a large and copious river. Its shore was full of lush greenery and wildlife.

Once the luggage was loaded, and all passengers were aboard, the ship's moorings were released and a shrill whistle of a siren was heard, started to navigate. The ship had a huge paddlewheel at the stern and a wide keel.

The Abosaid family watched as it slowly slid over the river, and how the port of Barranquilla gradually moved away. The heat suffocated them, and to relieve it, they stayed in the front, taking advantage of the breeze that refreshed them. There were Lebanese, Mexican, Dutch,

Spanish and even Asian passengers. Everyone had something in common; they were looking for a better future. Colombians were also aboard; many came from the Caribbean coast. People from those places seemed to be happier and uncomplicated.

With the passing of the hours, the trip became boring; the monotony and fatigue took over the environment. Most of the passengers spent time resting in reclining seats or in the hammocks that were hung on the ship's posts. They dealt with boredom by smoking or chatting about any triviality.

When the sun went down, some blood-hungry travelers appeared: different species of mosquitoes ready to attack their victims. A starry sky was the king of the night, the people were astonished by that wonder. The children played arming figures with those bright patches that could be seen in the distance. From time to time, and for an instant, some lightning would clear up the landscape.

It dawned and the air smelled of cocoa, announcing that breakfast was on its way: a cup of hot chocolate and a hard loaf of bread for the menu. There were no more stimulating options, despite the heat travelers felt. Eating that was the only alternative they had, because during the day they would only receive two meals, and lunch, would arrive at about five in the afternoon.

The passengers were unhappy, because the food was not very good, and the presence of those who served was dirty and neglected. They also felt the water they provided for bathing did not clean them, since it was yellow and had an unpleasant smell.

However, the discomfort caused by these issues was forgotten when you contemplated everything that monumental river offered on its way: crocodiles with their open jaws sunbathing on the banks of the river; alligators who slowly walked toward the water, and as they immersed their enormous bodies they made giant waves all around; white herons, in a masterful flight were crossing the river with pride.

Amid the vegetation, from time to time, they spotted a hut or a small town among the landscape. Some animals, such as pumas and jaguars, would camouflage themselves in the bushes when they heard the noise produced by the ship; others, like the monkeys, were seen doing mischief without shyness. Traveling on the "friendly river" as the early settlers called it, was like walking through a live encyclopedia.

***

The Abosaid family and the rest of the passengers arrived at *La Dorada,* in the middle Magdalena, there they took a seaplane that would take them to their final destination: Bogotá.

In the Colombian capital, their cousin Teresa received them with a smile and sweet words of welcome, she was accompanied by her son Carlos, an attractive young man who was attentive and collaborative all the time.

Antonio could not hide the emotion it invaded him, after understanding they were finally in Bogotá; they had managed to survive that adventure and now they would start a new life.

Initially, they were installed in an apartment owned by Carlos and it was located in the same place where the family business operated. They would be there only for a few days; then they would move to a home of the family in the Teusaquillo neighborhood.

Antonio and his family were closer than ever. He loved his wife with intensity. He knew all the sacrifices she had made following him. They were an example of a couple. He would do everything in his power so they never lack anything.

The Abosaid surname sounded in the most important circles of Bogotá; It was a clan who had managed to make a good fortune with the factory of leather gloves, women's clothing and silk stockings. While the children restarted their studies at the American College, Antonio began to work in the warehouse, he was in charge of the cash register. He did not earn much, but he could earn enough to support his family.

Everything was going well. It seemed that luck was smiling at them, until Carlos became infatuated with young Raquel, and this matter would end the peace and family harmony.

Rachel was very beautiful and in the prime of her youth; so, it was not surprising that Carlos might like her. He was a seductive but an unscrupulous man, who was married and had a family.

One afternoon, Carlos invited Raquel and Josefina to visit the hill of Monserrate, a place of peregrinate, where there is the church of *El Señor Caido de Monserrate.* To convince the girls, he assured them they would see all the city from above. But he had other intentions.

The young sisters were very innocent; in addition, they had been educated very strictly by their father Antonio. Despite this, they accepted their cousin's invitation. When they were returning home after the ride, Carlos stopped the car in an abandoned lot, and in front of Josefina, he wanted to kiss Rachel. Both were angered.

Josefina told him she would not allow such abuse. Carlos, to calm the girls, took a gift from a bag he had brought for Raquel, from the United States. She did not accept it. The two got out of the car and returned home walking, indignantly.

Raquel's rejection made Carlos feel humiliated; and to take revenge, he used tricks and falsehoods to dismiss Antonio from his work. And to complicate their lives even more, he demanded them to leave Teusaquillo's house.

After that, Antonio became a desperate man, he didn't know what to do, he had to get a house for his family, and he lacked the means to do so.

Fortunately, luck did not abandon them. During the time that Antonio worked in Carlos's warehouse, his children became well known in the neighborhood, so the boys made friends with young people of their age, neighbors of the sector.

Pepe, the oldest of the boys, had a very good friend, who, upon learning of the painful situation he and his family were going through, did not hesitate to tell his mother to help them. The good woman offered them a space inside their house to be housed for some time; in addition, she prepared another room that had street view, so that they could put up a shop and sell cigarettes, snacks and some delicious sweets, made with milk and muscovado sugar, which Rachel had learned to do in her spare time, known as *"panelitas"*.

——It must have been hard to face life, when the only relatives they had had left them adrift ——I said——, taking advantage that *Anwar* made a break to cool his throat and rest his voice.

——And all because of the meanness of Carlos who

saw nothing but his own complacency ——Charif replied, somewhat irritated; he also added:

——But my grandfather Antonio was not only brave, but also very optimistic and intelligent; to get their family to move ahead.

It was already *late* and even with the fire burning, the night felt very cold. *Anwar* felt tired, as did *Samir*; so, we decided it was time to put a stop on the story. We said good night and went to rest.

The sunrise on Mount Lebanon was beautiful. The sun gently warmed our skin. During lunch, we talked about our Abosaid grandparents and how Raquel set out to go to church every day to ask on her knees to get her family out of the difficult economic situation they were in.

***

Every day that passed I fell more in love with Lebanon, its people, its food and everything the country offered. I wasn't sure I wanted to go back to Colombia. But sooner or later we would have to lift anchors.

After dinner, like every night, we set out to continue listening to *Anwar*'s story, always translated by *Samir*:

——Antonio was still anguished because his family was going through many needs, he kept thinking about how he was going to solve his problems, because he couldn't find work easily. In the middle of his reflections, he decided to give luck a chance, and with some coins he found in an old coat, he bought a lottery ticket that he kept with hope. He kept it in the same pocket in which he had found the money.

Days later, on a foggy afternoon, he heard a loud uproar and the noise of some feet running, it was one of his children, he was coming in a hurry to tell him the number of his ticket had won. Antonio could not believe it. He jumped happily and the expression of his face changed from sad to cheerful, waving the ticket in the air he was screaming at everyone: I won!! I won the lottery prize!!

All his neighbors congratulated him. The woman who had given him a place to stay advised him to buy the building next to hers, assuring him it would be a good investment. Antonio listened to the lady, but did not pay much attention. At that time, he just wanted to return to Cuba. He was sure, that this time, he would do better there than in Bogotá. By then, he had not lost the link with aunt Juana, who insisted him to return. So, he did so.

A cold and rainy morning they all left behind the savanna of Bogotá and the hills it surrounded the city. After several days of traveling, and with an indescribable fatigue, they arrived at *Puerto Padre*. Antonio settled with his family in a quiet place which was located ten minutes from a sugar mill, not knowing that returning to Cuba was not the best of his decisions, because the socio-political conditions were changing and that was making life difficult over there.

The lottery money did not last long. Juana and Pedro borrowed him some of it to buy new furniture and other household items, and little by little, they spent it. Fortunately, Antonio managed to acquire the best panoramic camera of the time.

As for his children, none wanted to live in Cuba again, they spent their time crying and reneging, especially Raquel and her sister Feffa.

Raquel did not lose hope of returning to Colombia,

so she used to go to pray to *San Cayetano* every day, asking for the miracle of returning to Colombia. After eight months of continuous prayers, the miracle was conceded. Antonio took the most out of his camera, and for a living, turned to what he knew how to do well: to take pictures.

At that time, would not be only the official photographer of the Mayor, but a photographer of the ladies who belonged to the high society from Habana. Occupation, he performed successfully, and allowed him to support his family and giving him the opportunity to save some money. He knew his days in Cuba were counted; so, he made a photo album to demonstrate not only his work but also his talent.

Antonio, María and their children returned to the cold capital city of Colombia, Bogotá, eight months after having remained in Cuba. Antonio was full of enthusiasm and new projects; now, he knew he could work without relying on anyone. His camera, very modern for the time, would become the only one of its kind in the entire city. Without a doubt, life would bring them better opportunities.

Anwar concluded his story, giving the word to Charif, who assured he knew the rest of the story:

—According to Mom, a man named Víctor Villamil had the most important photographic studio in Bogotá; he was the one who gave Antonio Abosaid the opportunity to use his great camera. My grandfather learned a lot from Mr. Villamil and *vice versa;* furthermore, a friendship sprang up between them that would last the rest of their lives. Mr. Villamil made my grandfather to become an incredibly talented photographer.

Grandfather Antonio attended all university graduations and took with his lens, in a panoramic portrait, 1.60 cm long by 35 cm wide, groups of happy graduates; thus, little by little, he began to gain prestige and became the most famous photographer of the students graduations in Bogotá; consequently, the sale of copies of the photographs of the university students increased.

Over time, Carlos, the man who harmed my grandfather and his family so much during his first stay in Bogotá, offered uncle Alberto a job in his chain of stores. Between the two, what had happened in the past never came up again, to the contrary, they always had a very cordial relationship.

Over the years, uncle Alberto partnered with a friend and became independent by founding a store it sold the same line of women's clothing he was already accustomed to sell. By then Carlos ran the most prestigious female fashion brand factories in the country.

They were joined by aunt Lucy, who worked throughout her life with her brother. They prospered so much with the first warehouse, to later open a larger one in downtown of Bogotá, perhaps the most important of the time, in the city.

We must recognize Carlos was always the man who managed the business of the Abosaid family, until the day he was kidnapped and killed. It was one of the most difficult times for the clan.

Over the years, grandfather Antonio alternated photography with work in uncle Alberto's stores, because his job as a photographer only became active every six months, when university students graduated; for that reason, most of the year he was in charge of the cash register of one of the stores, always accompanied by his revolver Smith & Wesson caliber 32. My grandfather managed to be in that occupation almost until the age of seventy.

On her part, grandma Maria, from time to time, was also going to help her children in their different jobs. However, she always stood out, as an excellent woman, committed to the well-being of her family and very dedicated to household chores. I remembered her in her three-story house wearing her blue and white apron, adorned with little flowers.

In the middle of the kitchen of that house, there was a wooden table; that space was his domain. On that table she chopped, kneaded and prepared all the Lebanese dishes. As a child, I would stand up and sat on her legs while she continued kneading, or on a bench I had especially for me. I always watched her without losing detail while she cooked.

The rooms were on the third floor of the house. All single uncles lived with grandparents. The only ones who did not live there because they were married, was my mother and my aunt Josefina, even so, they always remained close to the paternal house. I visited my grandparents every day after school. How I adored them!

Life was routine. Grandfather Antonio in the warehouse cash register, my grandmother at home and his children making their own lives. As it happens in any family.

One day, unfortunately, grandma Maria became seriously ill and died of a diabetic coma at sixty. Sadness seized my grandfather. I remember him crying silently with his head down, in his armchair. He never thought about replacing my grandmother's absence with another woman; he decided to remain alone until death.

One night, at the age of eighty, he brought us all

together and told us he would travel to Lebanon. He wanted to sell some land he had inherited during his exile, because he did not want to lose them due to the absence of a claimant.

He left an early morning on a plane that would take him first to France and then to Lebanon. He stayed a few days in Paris, perhaps, remembering his time in that city when he was young and without a penny in his pocket. When he arrived in Lebanon, he contacted some acquaintances, sold his land, and bought some bracelets eighteen karat gold, forged by hand, to give his four daughters as a gift; jewels of an indescribable beauty they still keep.

My grandfather was a character. After the death of the grandmother, he left his job as a cashier and began to devote more time to photography; among other reasons, because he used to fall asleep in the cash register. Therefore, he thought to set up a photo lab in the house could give him something to do. Like him, I liked photography, and by that time, I had already done my first steps, so I stayed with him in the lab for hours helping him prepare chemicals.

Once, that we locked ourselves in the dark room, I was using a wrist watch which became fluorescent in the dark, when my grandfather noticed it, he was horrified, he shouted at me to take it off, more worried than angry, because he said it would ruin the negatives. I immediately went out and took it off. Later on, I found out that this wouldn't harm the chemicals.

Grandpa was always a very elegant man. He liked to wear a tie and vest; he constantly rolled up the sleeves of his shirt, as a sign he was ready to prepare his delicious Lebanese recipes or when he was going to enter his photo lab. He always used a gold clover with a small diamond in the center, as a tie clip.

During my adolescence, when I became a rebel, my grandfather scolded me. My aunts laughed because of his sermons.

He liked to talk to me, and at the end of the afternoon; he asked me to sit next to him and offered me a *whiskey,* he said I should learn how to drink properly, as we were drinking, he used to tell me all his stories and adventures.

He never liked driving or being transported for he didn't want to feel invalid, so to get to the warehouse where he worked as a cashier for so many years, he used to take the bus which left him right in front of the door of the place. Then he returned on the same bus.

At ninety-nine, the unavoidable passage of time acted; it him fall on the stairs and fracture his hip. It was the beginning of the end. I prepared myself for the unavoidable, therefore, I decided to pay him a tribute for his work as a photographer throughout his life. It was a real surprise for him.

Reluctantly, I took him out of his bed and sat him in the wheelchair, with tricks, I took him to the gallery where the photographic material was exhibited, the product of many years of work.

When he entered the gallery and saw all his exposed photographs, he opened his mouth in disbelief. He was stunned. Friends and family appeared and surrounded him with and endless applause. His photographs, and so many happy memories, made tears run down his cheeks. I was happy and very excited.

I had invited the press to the tribute; in this way, reporters from various media press interviewed him and congratulated him on his great career. He was recognized by everyone as one of the most important men of the moment. In life he earned the respect and admiration of many. The least I could do for him was to honor him. He deserved it. He was a great man and an excellent photographer.

After the tribute, grandfather Antonio began to decline more each day. One night I entered his bedroom and found him delirious; between Arabic and Spanish, he talked to his mother, his brothers and grandmother Maria, and told them he would soon be reunited with them.

When I heard it, a sharp pain pierced my heart. I felt a sadness so deep I could hardly recover. I knew he would die soon. The only thing it comforted me was to think that many of his loved ones would be on the other side waiting for him. Shortly after, he expired.

We all congregate at home. One by one we pass in front of him and kiss his cold cheek. Pain seized the place. We cried for a long time.

One rainy afternoon, I said goodbye to grandpa Antonio. And thanked to God because I could enjoy him for so many years. He was my friend, my great example. He was an adventurous, brave man, who loved life dearly, to his wife and all his offspring.

EPILOGUE

——Charif, I have a lump in my throat. I don't know how to tell you, but I want to go to Beirut ——I said. After the war many children have run out of parents. I think I can help them by getting a home in Bogotá, so I want to take pictures. There are so many mothers who cannot have children and would like to adopt. I will be like the Consul the grandfather talked about in his stories, who wanted to help his nationals who landed in distant lands.

——See, we have to go back.

——I know we must go to Beirut, but it will be only to buy the tickets to go back.

——It will be only a few days. No more than a week, I promise you ——I begged.

——It's fine, but only one, and nothing more than one ——he said a little angry.

The next day we left Mount Lebanon towards Beirut in the old Toyota of *Samir*. Everything was calm. That nightmare seemed to be over, however, there was a lot of vigilance on the roads.

Upon entering the city, we went straight to the hotel we had stayed in during the war; its owner welcomed us with open arms. The hotel was being rebuilt; it looked the same as we saw it for the first time.

Like the hotel, Beirut was under reconstruction. Its leader had promised a new city where no one was missing housing or food. The people admired him and loved him like a father.

After buying the tickets, I begged Charif to take me to where the children were; I wanted to visit them, I felt a need in my soul, I wanted to see how I could help them, what I could do for those creatures.

When I entered the field, I was greatly impressed. My legs faltered. I felt like I was going to fall apart. I sat on a bench to cry, I couldn't take it anymore, my heart was going to explode with sadness. I cleaned the sea of tears from my face, and, with pleading eyes, asked Charif to adopt one of the orphans. That thought had already passed through my mind, but I was afraid Charif would not support me.

When the children saw me, they ran towards me; they grabbed my skirt without wanting to let go. They smiled hopefully. At that moment I did not know what to do, I was touched by all the love that came out from those innocent hearts. I would have liked to adopt them all, but I could only welcome one; and that decision would be guided by my heart, which would be my best guide.

Charif surprised me. He never told me I was crazy; on the contrary, he supported me unconditionally. He also felt the need to adopt a child, I knew that God had allowed us to continue living because we had a mission to accomplished: to give a home to an orphan child. It was the best way to thank God.

We contacted the people in charge of the place and informed them what we wanted.

There was no problem; our request was accepted. Walking with Charif among the group of children we saw a little girl coloring in a notebook. Slowly, I approached her. I did not need to convince myself. I knew she was the one we would choose when I saw her gaze, filled with hope, staring at us she was asking in silent to take her with us. I had no doubt.

Charif agreed. The managers told us that *Aisha* was a very special little girl. One of them called her. The girl approached slowly, as if sensing what would happen. Her expression was a bit cold, but her smile was like seeing a sky.

I introduced myself and asked her name. She answered me in a soft voice, we could hardly hear. Charif carried her in his arms. He looked good being a father. Aisha stroked her hair with her little fingers; in Arabic she pronounced two words that we understood perfectly: *Mom, Dad.*

We return to Mount Lebanon with our daughter and *Samir*. When *Anwar* found out about our decision, he was very happy. That night Aisha was smiling with more joy. She kept talking to *Anwar* and *Samir*. Undoubtedly, she was a very nice girl.

Our departure was approaching. We had formed such an intense emotional bond that we considered *Anwar* and *Samir*, part of our family. The days we were at their home had been very special. Their company comforted us during the postwar period, and in addition, they had done something very valuable for us: they gave us the treasure which represented the life of the Abosaid's grandparents. It was inevitable not to love them.

The farewell was tremendously touched. *Anwar* and *Samir* hugged us recommending us to return. Aisha gave them three kisses on each cheek. She was a sweetie, we also wrapped them with hugs and kisses. We promised them we would return soon, not only for we had found thanks to them, the story we had so longed for; but, because in Lebanon, our love had grown and embodied in the greatest fortune: our daughter *Aisha*.

THE END

Dear reader:

Thank you for having read my work, I hope you enjoyed it. I invite you to read my other novels:

Who Killed Veronika? The Last Lebanese, The Kindergarten–Stories of Yesterday, Abadón-Judgment and Punishment

If you want to know more about me or contact me, I leave you the following links:

email: annasimonlibros@gmail.com

Facebook: @ ANNASIMONLIBROS
Facebook: Club de lectores de Anna Simón

Website: www.annasimonescritora.com